THE

TROJAN

WAR

MUSEUM

# THE
# TROJAN
# WAR
# MUSEUM

AND OTHER STORIES

Ayşe Papatya Bucak

**W. W. NORTON & COMPANY**

*Independent Publishers Since 1923*

New York | London

For information about permission to reproduce selections from this book, write to Permissions, W. W. Norton & Company, Inc., 500 Fifth Avenue, New York, NY 10110

For information about special discounts for bulk purchases, please contact W. W. Norton Special Sales at specialsales@wwnorton.com or 800-233-4830

Manufacturing by Sheridan
Book design by Chris Welch
Production manager: Beth Steidle

Library of Congress Cataloging-in-Publication Data

Names: Bucak, Ayse Papatya, author.
Title: The Trojan War Museum and other stories / Ayse Papatya Bucak.
Description: First edition. | New York : W. W. Norton & Company, 2019.
Identifiers: LCCN 2018057459 | ISBN 9781324002970 (hardcover)
Classification: LCC PS3602.U225 T76 2019 | DDC 813/.6—dc23
LC record available at https://lccn.loc.gov/2018057459

W. W. Norton & Company, Inc., 500 Fifth Avenue, New York, N.Y. 10110
www.wwnorton.com

W. W. Norton & Company Ltd., 15 Carlisle Street, London W1D 3BS

1 2 3 4 5 6 7 8 9 0

*for my parents,*

MARGOT AND SÜREYYA BUCAK,

*who could be separated into my American half*

*and my Turkish half but are really*

*so much more*

# CONTENTS

# THE HISTORY OF
# GIRLS

›››————————————————————→

**W**hile we waited we were visited by the ghosts of the girls who had already died. Those who were closest to the explosion, in the kitchen sneaking butter and bread when the gas ignited, the ones who died immediately, in a sense without injury, the girls who died explosively.

The dead girls waited with us, amidst the rubble, our heads pillowed on it, our arms and legs canopied by it, some of us punctured by it. The rubble was heavy, of course. The weight of it made us wonder what happened to the softer things. Our sheets and blankets, our letters from home, our Korans, our class notes, the slips of paper we exchanged throughout the day, expressing our affections and disaffections for each other, for our teachers, for the rituals of our contained life. What about the curtains on our windows? we thought. The stories and poems we read to each other at night or the ones we kept private, folded in our pockets? What about our pockets? Our uniforms, our gym skirts, our head scarves and stockings? The too soft pillows we always complained of? The ones the oldest girls hoarded, sleeping with three or four stacked under their cheeks even though their heads sank into the too soft centers and their necks ached in the morning. The explosion, it seemed, turned everything to stone. Except us. We were soft then, softer than we ever were.

Have you ever seen a buzzard? They are all feathers and fat, not like skeletons at all, but soft like cushions. Except for their beaks and claws.

THERE WERE DAY GIRLS and night girls. Day girls went home at three o'clock, swept their mothers' houses, helped their mothers cook *köfte* and pilaf, slept in beds with their sisters, with their brothers and mothers and fathers in nearby rooms. There were more than a hundred of them; sometimes we confused the names of the youngest. But there were only fourteen of us: older girls in the room on the right, younger girls in the room on the left. Not a door to close in between, so all night long we heard each other giggle and snore and cry and dream and sometimes we shouted into the dark, goodnightgoodnightgoodnight.

The day girls were curious about us, of course. And we about them. But there was always a difference: at night, day girls had mothers and night girls had each other.

There were Açelya and Seda, Samime and Hamiyet, Rabia, Türkan, and finally Fadime, the baby, seven years old on the day she'd arrived, only two months earlier. Ghosts.

And then there were Mualla, Latife, Zehra, Sahiba, Nuray, Gül, and Celine. Waiting.

How could we all hear each other? It was like we were on our own radio channel, each with a clear signal.

THE DEAD GIRLS were from the room on the left: the oldest only twelve. Usually we were the ones to sneak into the kitchen, usually they were the ones to sleep through. How many nights had they copied us without our noticing? How many nights would we, could we, bear the guilt?

We could not see them, and yet there they were. Between the darkness of night and the building's collapse and the bright ring of the explosion still sounding in our heads, we could not see much. Instead we felt the light fingertips of the dead girls' touch, and heard their high voices saying, "Does this tickle? Won't you laugh? How about this? Does this tickle?"

"Stop it," we said. "We don't want to be tickled." But they wouldn't stop it and it did tickle just a little. So we laughed and they did, too.

"Help is coming," the dead girls said. "People are waking."

"Who?" we asked.

"People," the dead girls said.

We called out the names of the night janitor and his wife and even their fat baby, but they did not answer.

"What happened?" we asked one after another until finally the dead girls told us. Naturally it was expected they would know things we didn't.

It was what we had long suspected. The gas. The dormitory was always too hot or too cold, depending on what had gone wrong with the gas. Something was always wrong with the gas, and the teachers would adjust it only to turn the heat to cold or the cold to heat. At night when the teachers went to their homes and the day girls went to their homes and the cooks and the cleaners and the gardener went to their homes and we were left only with the night janitor and his wife and their fat baby, we curled under our blankets, sometimes three to a bed, as if our bodies had any heat left to share, or we slept on the tiled floor of the hall with our limbs slung out, as if we could separate from ourselves and become cooler.

FIRST IT WAS DARK and quiet, later it was bright and loud. First there were dead girls and living girls; later there were girls in between. We would have lingered even there, stars poking through the rubble, cold ground beneath us, cold air creeping in, but with blood in our hearts and air in our chests. We would have stayed there as long as we could even with the dead girls saying, "It's not so bad. I didn't feel a thing. And look, now I can fly."

THE YOUNGEST WAS SEVEN, the oldest nineteen, though most girls left school before then, to return home, to the east or the west, before marrying. Sometimes a husband they knew, sometimes not. Some girls went to university, abroad or at home, you shouldn't think they didn't; we were not the girls that you might assume. We did not wear our head scarves over our eyes. Some girls went to work. Some girls stayed on as teachers. The school had a long line of girls who did many things deep into the past and far into the future.

———————

SOME OF US CRIED, of course. The dead girls tried to comfort us, but our tears were no longer ours to control. And when the dead girls tried to unpin our arms and legs, to move the rubble that held us in place, they found they had only their ordinary strength. And when they tried to hold our hands, stroke our hair, as we so often comforted each other after our petty fights, we found their touch had grown as hot as a lit match tip.

"Stop it," we yelled. "That hurts."

"Sorry," the dead girls said. "We didn't know."

"Sorry," we said back, "we didn't mean to yell." How courteous we all became while we waited.

"Are they still coming?" we asked. "When are they coming?"

"They're coming," the dead girls said. "As fast as they can."

"Hold on," they said. "They're coming."

"Look how pretty you look," they told us. "I can't believe it. In the middle of such a disaster, you still look so pretty."

"Thanks," we said. Or, "Don't be ridiculous." We blushed and we giggled, we did all the things we always did. They were our best friends.

"How do we look?" the dead girls asked. "Are we wearing clothes? Do we have wings?"

But we didn't know; in the dark, we couldn't see a thing.

"I SEE A LIGHT," Mualla yelled. "Look at the light." And first we thought she had been rescued, or even dug her way out as some of us had been trying to do, but then she died.

"Hello," she said, and the dead girls chorused back, "Hello, Mualla."

"Where did you go?" we asked her and "What is it like?" But all she would say was "I saw a light." She was just the kind of girl to tell you what you already knew.

Have you ever had a hawk's shadow cross over you? It happened sometimes when we were in the garden with our potatoes. It is like death's cape sweeping swiftly over your head. Every time we screamed.

THE SEARCHERS, when they came, turned on a spotlight. It shone through the rubble, a moonlight spotlight, leaving us blinded by light rather than dark. It was a light so sharp it should have cut through the rubble like a laser, and yet it was as heavy as a stone. We felt pushed into the earth like seeds poked too far underground.

The searchers called our names, the living and the dead— they didn't know the difference yet. Sometimes we recognized their voices: our teachers, the school nurse, the doctor who came to check us twice a year. Others were voices we had rarely heard, of people whose names we had never learned: the baker who made the cookies we liked to buy when we were taken into town, the men who came and collected our garbage, the repairmen who fixed our leaks and painted our walls, the old man who delivered the ill-fated gas, accidental executioner. Then there were the voices of the day girls woken from their beds at home, and the voices of their parents and their brothers and sisters. How happy they sounded, how excited. How could they help it? Our mothers, of course, lived far away. Perhaps they knew what was happening, perhaps it was on the news already, perhaps they woke in the night and felt, Something's not right.

Would we be mothers, we wondered. Or would we always be girls?

"Precious, precious," we heard someone wail until they were all saying it: "Precious, precious."

We called back at first, a chorus of the dead and the living, but the searchers never seemed to hear, and soon there was only the sound of shovels and machines, and digging that never came closer.

We were like diamonds waiting to be dug out.

"Precious, precious," one of the dead girls mocked until we begged her to stop.

"OH," CELINE SAID, a minor expression of surprise, uncharacteristically quiet, as she joined the dead girls.

"Hello, Celine," they said.

"I TOLD ALLAH I WAS ANGRY," Fadime, our baby, called out. "I told him he was evil for killing the Chinese boys and girls who had no brothers and sisters. You are all my punishment," she cried. "Allah got angry with me because I got angry with him."

After the earthquakes in China we wrote letters expressing our sympathies and sent them to the newspaper. After the Indonesian tsunami we wrote letters too, but we did not know where to send them so we buried them in the earth next to the potatoes. After the earthquakes in Greece, we prayed every night, and when there were earthquakes in Istanbul we gathered the small sums of money we had saved for buying cookies when we were taken into town and mailed them to the government.

"Oh, Fadime," we said. "Allah forgave you right away. It's not your fault, nor his."

"I don't believe, and you shouldn't either," Celine said. "I'm dead now and I see no signs of heaven. You should all do what you want and not worry about being cursed."

She was always in trouble anyway, we thought to ourselves. What would she have done differently if she'd known there was no heaven?

"I heard that," Celine said, and we cried out, "You see, you are a miracle. This is no time for doubt."

"This is exactly the time for doubt," Celine said. "Why didn't anybody fix the gas?"

She was only half Turkish. Her mother was French and she'd sent Celine to a boarding school in Switzerland, but then her mother died and her father brought her here. He did not think to sort her things, and so she brought *Tintin* and *Madeline* and a book with dirty pictures drawn in ink. Also a Superman comic. Maybe she brought the devil, too. What did it matter to us then?

But why didn't anybody fix the gas? Surely that did not require an act of God.

"Maybe we're angels," Fadime said.

"Maybe we aren't *dead*-dead, only in between," another of the dead girls said.

"I just want to be *dead*-dead," Açelya cried. "I feel so tired."

"Me, too," the other dead girls said. "I feel so tired."

"Where are the rescuers?" we asked. It was always up to us to distract them.

"Coming," the dead girls said, quiet again. "Can't you hear them digging?"

We were quiet, but we couldn't hear.

Have you ever pulled a potato from the ground before it was ready? It looks like a thing that has been alive too long.

"I SEE MY MOTHER," Celine said.

"Where?" the other dead girls cried.

"Inside of me," Celine said. "She is an angel inside of an angel."

"Celine," we said. "Stop it. They are only little girls."

"Tell us what she looks like," the dead girls said.

They never were ones to know when they were being teased.

"Don't, Celine," we warned.

"She has one eye hanging out of her head and there are rotten worms coming out of her ears and she has a broken leg. I can see the bone sticking out of her rotten skin."

The dead girls were hysterical then. They could not be contained. "I see her, too. Oh, she's hideous. Oh, I'm scared."

Last year they all got rashes. Last month they all saw UFOs. Before long the ghosts would all be seeing ghosts.

"Celine," we said, "we told you not to."

WE HAD BEEN TAUGHT the history of girls. In Hiroshima, hundreds of schoolgirls were clearing homes and roads to make the widest of fire lanes when the bomb came. In China, in India, some girls weren't allowed to live a day. In Russia, in

Uzbekistan, in Georgia, in Ukraine, girls were sold once and shipped abroad to be sold again and again. It was how we learned our geography. The history of innocents.

But we learned, too, the history of sinners. Girls who were stoned by their villagers. Burned by their brothers. Killed by their fathers. Cast out by their mothers. Our lessons were full of girls who died. Stoned for this and stoned for that. More geography. In Afghanistan in Somalia in Florida in Iran and Iraq and Egypt and Syria. Be good, we were told. Legs tight, lips tight, eyes open, mouths closed.

Gül was sent to school because her brother threatened to kill her for having a boyfriend. Açelya was sent because it was her best chance to go to law school. All of us were sent to school to be girls, to be protected until we were women. Girlhood, we were taught, was something to be survived.

Maybe, we thought, the world needs enemies it can love, enemies who are no threat at all. Maybe, we thought, that is the story inside the history of girls.

"We are virgin sacrifices," Celine called out.

"Oh hush, Celine," we said.

AT NIGHT WE HAD TOLD TALES. The Somalian girl turned to stone before the attackers' stones hit her, and as the stones bounced to her feet, flakes of dust rose from her, and when she turned back to flesh, she had only cuts and bruises and aches and pains. The Egyptian girl shot lasers out of her turned-to-ruby eyes and blinded her attackers. The Syrian girls turned to water, drowned their attackers, turned back to flesh, laid out the drowned bodies and, when the bodies were dry, lit them on fire. In Afghanistan, girls rose up to the sun and hid it from the sky until their attackers turned to ice.

But don't think we wanted to be boys. Boys seemed lonely. Boys seemed helpless. Eventually, if we were boys, we would be expected to be cruel, at least once, if not every day. We just wanted those girls to be strong.

"CELINE, TELL US ABOUT the dancing princesses," the dead girls said.

If we had never stolen snacks in the night, then they never would have copied us.

"I won't," Celine said. "I don't like that story anymore."

"We need it. We're scared. We're tired. We need it," they chorused.

They were so much as they ever were.

"You don't."

"We do."

"You don't."

"Oh, Celine," we said. "Can't you just humor them?"

"Why should I? They aren't babies anymore."

"Then do it for us," we said. "We are scared and tired, too. We need it, too."

"Well, then you're all babies," she said. And then: "Fine. Once there were twelve sisters and they never wanted to sleep and so they didn't, they danced. They danced all night and wore out their shoes and their father never knew why so he killed a bunch of princes trying to find out until one got help—totally unfairly of course—from some old hag and that prince followed the princesses and he danced and drank their drinks and had their fun and then he told on them and ruined everything."

"Celine!" the dead girls chorused. "Tell it right."

"Please, Celine," we said. And: "Where are the rescuers? Why can't we hear them?"

"They're there," Celine said softly. "They're coming."

"For you," she added.

What was the fairy-tale future we hoped for? That we would turn to stone and be protected? That we would shoot lasers out of our turned-to-ruby eyes or that we would turn the world to ice and kill our enemies? Who would want such a thing? Those stories were no help to us then.

All we hoped for were lives of promise and fulfillment and to be released into heaven at the end of time. What we wanted was to live just a little longer. What we wanted was to be together.

"Please, Celine," we said.

"All right, are you ready?" Celine asked.

"Yes, yes," we said.

"All right. Once there was and once there wasn't, in the time of princes and princesses and genies and jinn and boys turned to men and girls turned to women, in that time there were twelve sisters. And they loved to dance. Each night their father, the Sultan, would lock them in their room—twelve beds, twelve sisters, all in a row—and each morning, he'd turn the key to find them still sleeping, but with twelve pairs of shoes, worn through, at the foot of their beds.

"'Your shoes,' he'd cry each morning. 'What are you doing to your shoes?'

"'Good morning, Baba,' the girls would say, each in turn, youngest to oldest, and they would run, barefoot, to kiss him and hug him and not ever answer his question.

"Then one morning he said, 'You must stop this. Your mother is weeping. The princes are weeping. The cobbler is weeping. He has threatened to kill himself if he has to make any more shoes.'

"'Tell him not to cry, Baba,' the oldest daughter said. 'We don't even like shoes. He need not make us any more.'

"'Yes,' her sisters echoed. 'He need not make us any more,' and the youngest daughter started a pirouette on her bare toes, but the oldest caught her in her arms. 'Not now,' she whispered in the youngest daughter's ear."

"CELINE, YOU'RE STILL NOT telling it right," Fadime said.

"Shush," we told her. "Let us find out what happens."

"THE COBBLER KILLED HIMSELF," Celine said, and we could hear her lips press tight.

"Oh, Celine," we said. "He didn't."

"I don't want him to," Fadime cried.

"Fine," Celine said, "he didn't kill himself but he refused to make any more shoes and so the girls had to dance bare-foot and the next morning when their father woke them he found their sheets soaked in blood and their toes worn down to nubs."

"Celine!" we cried out.

"The daughters could not walk so they spent the rest of their lives in bed where nurses brought them food and drink and they peed in pots that were kept under their beds and they even got married in bed and their husbands, all princes, lay in bed next to them. Twelve big beds all in a row."

"I don't want to grow up!" Mualla cried out.

"Don't worry, you won't," Celine said.

"Oh, Celine," we said. "You don't have to be so mean."

"I'm not mean," she said.

"You're selfish," we said. "We all know it."

"I'm not selfish," Celine said. "Say it. I'm not selfish."

"Celine," we said.

"Please, I'm not," she said.

She was and she wasn't; we all knew that.

There was a pause and a stifled hiccup or sob and Celine said, "Tell my brother I'm sorry I stole his Fenerbahçe jersey."

We were quiet, until Gül said, "I'll tell him."

There was another pause and another stifled hiccup or sob.

Then Sahiba said, "But are you sorry?"

Celine often wore the jersey under her uniform or slept with it in her arms as if it were a stuffed animal. We had even named it Mehmet after her favorite player.

We giggled.

She giggled.

"Maybe not," she said. "Maybe you should tell him it was a comfort to me."

"We will," we said. "We'll tell him."

"Yes, yes," the others said. "Tell my brother my sister my mother my father my aunt my grandmother my best friend from when I was five the boy I never talked to the boy I never met the husband I would have had the children I would have had tell them we are sorry we love them we are all right we will never forget them never forget us. Tell them."

"Yes," we said. "We will tell them. Unless you tell them first."

"Everyone be quiet," Celine said, and we could not help but smile. "Once there was and once there wasn't," she said, "in the time when genies were jinn and children remained children and nobody was born and nobody died, in the time when the earth stood still and the sun shone bright, in that time, there were fourteen princesses. And they loved to dance. They danced all night when they were meant to be sleeping, and then in the morning when they slept they dreamt of dancing. Night and day, they spun and spun, circling round and round, arms out wide and arms at their sides, spinning wider and wider until they could not even be seen.

"'Aren't you tired,' people would cry at the fourteen dancing princesses but inside the dance the fourteen princesses saw only each other and heard only each other and they spun and they spun and they never stopped spinning and their feet never hurt and their heads never hurt and their hearts never hurt. Inside their circle, they spun and they never stopped, not ever, not to grow old and not to die and not to work and not to marry and not to have children and not to eat bread and butter or sleep in the cold or the hot, not to do anything but spin. Together. Always."

She was quiet and so were we.

"Thank you, Celine," we said.

"I don't care," she said, but we knew she did.

"You're not selfish," we said. "We didn't mean it."

"We're spinning, we're spinning," the dead girls said. "Watch me," Fadime said. "Can you see me spinning?"

"Yes," we said, though of course we couldn't.

The history of girls is always told as a tragedy. Growing old is a tragedy and so is dying young.

WHAT, WE HAD ALWAYS asked each other, could it be like to be stoned? Were girls pelted like the stray dogs we saw being chased away with rocks by shopkeepers? Was it like dodge-ball, which our American teacher made us play in the yard until only Celine was left standing and we all refused to play ever again because she was so vicious? Was it like the snowball fights we read about in books? Or was it more like being hit with a hammer, close and bloody? Maybe it was the weight of human hatred that knocked girls from their feet.

Once we tossed rocks at each other just to see, but we missed every time.

SOMETIMES WE FELL QUIET. Sometimes another girl died. She would let out a small sound or a loud one, death still a surprise, even under the circumstances.

"Hello," the other girls would say, as if she had entered a room they were in. There were so many more of them then.

HOW HARD IT IS to explain, what it was like. We were together, as we were so accustomed to being. We made our present worth living, as we so often had. But then the rescue took so much longer than we expected.

"OH, WE'RE ON TELEVISION," the dead girls said. "There are cameras and reporters and even Americans."

"What can you see?" we asked but the dead girls wouldn't say.

"Are our parents there?" we asked but the dead girls wouldn't say.

"Are you still there?" we called out and they did not answer.

What is the heaviest thing you can imagine? A boulder? A house? An airplane? In all of the world, what is the heaviest thing? Can you even imagine it?

"Where are you?" we asked.

But they did not answer.

How quickly it happened then. One girl, then another. Gone.

"PLEASE," I SAID, "don't leave me."

"Where are you?" I asked. "Can't I come, too?"

"Please," I said. "Precious," I said. "Precious."

But they did not answer.

"I hate you," I said. "You are all mean."

"Take me with you," I yelled. "Please take me with you."

And from somewhere I could not see and in voices I could barely hear, they said, "Oh Zehra, don't be silly" and "We'll miss you. Don't forget to tell them" and "Goodnightgoodnightgoodnight."

"I don't want to grow up without you," I said.

But they did not answer. And though my arms were at my sides, and my legs were beneath me in a way they never should be, and my voice could not be heard, and my eyes could not see, I felt twice over that I always would be—and I never would be—without them.

Have you ever seen a girl?

She is my history.

# A CAUTIONARY TALE

>>>————————————————————→

In the last years of the nineteenth century, the third-strongest man in the world was said to be a Turk named Yusuf Ismail, known in his homeland as Yusuf the Great or Yusuf the Large, and known everywhere else as the Terrible Turk. He was the first of a line of legendary, savage, monstrously large wrestlers all called, one after the other, the Terrible Turk.

It's true some of the Terrible Turks were fakes, not actually Turks at all. And though later some would say Yusuf Ismail was a French dockworker in a fez with nothing more than an out-of-control appetite and the ability to spike men into the ground so hard they could not rise without help, he was indeed a Turk, a sultan's favorite, born in a corner of the then-immense Ottoman Empire, and though he was in the end perhaps a showman, maybe even a stooge, he also once was a hero and a champion.

When he was six years old, Yusuf could pin twelve-year-olds to the grass in less than a minute. When he was twelve, he could pin full-grown men using just his legs, and by the time he was thirteen, nobody in his village would spar with him. He had to strengthen his fingers by kneading balls of mud, his legs and arms by pushing on walls of stone, and his shoulders by hoisting fallen trees. By fourteen, he was never seen without a large and heavy object in his hands.

By then he was already the village champion, and he traveled regularly to competitions at weddings and other festivals, where he was matched against other village champions, all older and more experienced, and they would lean on each other for hours, testing for the smallest sign of weakness. It was then, when Yusuf was not yet the biggest or the strongest, and his matches seemed as if they would never end, that his skills and his fame grew. He had great patience then. He knew how to push men muscle by muscle until finally they fell.

By the time a French manager found him and imported him to Europe, he was already the head wrestler of the Ottoman Empire, thirty-seven years old, six foot two, 250 pounds. Not so big now, but big then. Twenty pounds heavier than his average opponent.

It took him four seconds to win his first European match, in which he lifted the French champion, Sabès, by the throat, then turned the Frenchman upside down and held him at arm's length while he twisted and turned.

It's said the Turk had no neck and that was why Strangler Lewis, the American heavyweight champion, could not defeat him. It's said it took six men, three on each arm, to stop the Turk from killing one of his opponents.

It's said he promised to cut his own throat if he was ever beaten.

It's said he had a dagger in his turban even when on the mat.

It's said that he had a cruel face, that he ate ten times a day and never paid for a meal, that he had a childish love of finery, that he had a sluggish Oriental brain, that he did not understand paper money, that he liked the shine and clink of gold coins. That he was once a bandit.

It's true he wore his gold belted around his waist. Eight thousand dollars on the day he died. Or maybe ten. Or maybe five. At least forty pounds in weight, anyway.

And it's true he drowned, just months after the fight at Madison Square Garden, along with nearly six hundred other passengers and crew, when the French ocean liner *La Bourgogne* hit the British ship *Cromartyshire* on the American Independence Day, just on the edge of the nineteenth century, July 4, 1898. They died, all of them, off the coast of Nova Scotia, in the North Atlantic, while the ship was on its way to Le Havre, where Yusuf was to join his wife and two children, so that they could travel home together.

It's said the Terrible Turk refused to remove his belt full of gold when the ship went down, and he leapt, dagger in hand, onto a lifeboat full of mothers and children, dropping it deep into the sea.

It's said he wailed from the ship's rail begging Allah to save him.

It's said he fell into the water and tried to lift himself onto a lifeboat, rocking the craft so severely with his great weight that a crewman first tried to push him away with an oar and, when that failed, took an axe and cut off each of the Terrible Turk's grasping hands, the Turk's grip so tight that his hands remained clinging to the lip of the boat while his body and his gold sank into the sea.

WHEN YOU WERE A CHILD, *did you find that story credible?*
  *When I was a child I didn't know what "credible" meant.*
  *It means believable.*
  *I know what it means now.*
  *Did you find the story believable as a child?*
  *I think most people would do anything to save their lives.*
  *Did you think that when you were a child?*
  *I have no idea.*
  *So now, you think Yusuf Ismail was just trying to save his own life?*
  *I was referring to the crewman. Who cut off his hands.*
  *You think the crewman cut off Yusuf Ismail's hands in order to save his own life?*
  ——

  *You don't think the crewman was trying to save the lives of the women and children on his boat?*
  ——

  *So, did you find the story believable as a child?*
  *I don't recall.*
  *But you find it believable now?*
  *I think it's possible.*
  *Probable?*

*Possible.*

*Does the probability of the story's veracity——its truth——influence its effect on you?*

*I know what "veracity" means. And I said, it's possible, not probable.*

*Does the possibility of the story's veracity influence its effect on you?*

*The story has no effect on me.*

*Why not?*

*Why should it?*

*Some would find that a sad story. Or a story from which something could be learned.*

*Well, I don't.*

*Why do you think that story is told to children?*

*Because it's entertaining, I suppose.*

*Not to teach them a lesson?*

*Yes, I suppose to teach them a lesson.*

*And what is that lesson?*

*To be ashamed of themselves.*

*You think that is the intended lesson?*

*Maybe not intended, no.*

*But that story makes you feel ashamed of yourself?*

——

*As a child, did it make you feel ashamed of yourself?*

*No, it gave me nightmares.*

*Why?*

*Because of the hands, of course. The way they cut off his hands.*

*Why does that story make you feel ashamed?*

*It doesn't.*

*It doesn't make you feel ashamed?*

*No, it doesn't.*

*But you think its lesson is to make children feel ashamed when they hear it?*

*Not all children.*

*Which children?*

*Turkish children, of course. The terrible Turkish children.*

*You don't think Yusuf Ismail was a hero?*

*I don't really care one way or the other.*

## The Fight at Madison Square Garden
## New York City, 1898
## Four months before he died

At the time, Madison Square Garden could seat eight thousand and stand a thousand more. On the night Ernest Roeber fought the Terrible Turk, perhaps another two hundred crowded their way in. There were five matchups, but it was clear that all nine thousand, two hundred men and women of the crowd were there for the main event. They each had the air of fighters, sweating, shouting, impatient, and often indignant. Fights broke out, men screamed, women fainted, some were nearly trampled.

The Terrible Turk was believed to be honest, unwilling to lose, and therefore unwilling to fix matches. It was meant to be a return to glory for the oldest sport among men.

No holds were barred. American Greco-Roman rules.

The Turk wore a turban of plaid.

A fall had to be made on the mat to count. The best two out of three falls would earn the winner five hundred dollars and half of the gate.

There was no rope, no posts, no ring, really. Just a mat on a stage, six feet above the crowd, only that height separating the fighters from their audience.

The Turk was six inches the taller.

They shook hands at the start.

Reporters lifted their notebooks, the referee took his stance, trainers and managers and people all across the arena planted their feet as if the fight depended on their ability to keep their balance.

The Turk could throw a man to the mat with such force that the fall alone knocked him out.

He wrenched men's necks so badly that for days they could not look straight ahead.

But Roeber was one of the most popular champions of the past twenty years. A handsome man. A crowd favorite.

On the first move, without ceremony, seemingly without effort, Roeber was dropped, so fast that to the people seated at the top of the arena, who could not see where he lay, it was as if he had vanished. But just as fast, Roeber leapt to his feet and then off the mat and out of the field of play. If there had been a rope, a ring, Roeber would have been outside it, and if the Turk dropped him there, the fall wouldn't count.

There Roeber stayed, orbiting the mammoth Turk, still in the center. "Fight!" one man in the crowd yelled. "Fight!" But nobody took up his chant. Periodically the Turk leaned forward and tried to swat Roeber back onto the mat, but the champion stayed on his feet, just out of reach. Finally the Turk, too, stepped off the mat, grabbed Roeber's face in his two hands, and tried to lift him back into the field of play. But Roeber wiggled and writhed, and soon he was free, orbiting again. It was only seconds later that the Turk grabbed him once more, harder this time, and pushed him, threw him really, off the platform, so that Roeber dropped six feet to the ground below, landing first on his shoulder and then on his head, unconscious.

The audience thought he was dead. A madness overtook them. Words frothed out of their mouths. "Kill him!" they screamed.

The Turk looked out at them, used his long fingers to mimic Roeber's running around the ring, pointed to his own chest, then pantomimed two men wrestling. He seemed to hold a match in his own imagination. Not my fault, his fingers seemed to say. Police surrounded the platform, and the Turk was led away, saying in Arabic and then French, "I only want to fight."

The Turk was in his dressing room when the match was declared for Roeber.

The *New York Times* called him "almost frenzied with anger."

"Kill the Turk!" "Lynch him!" the *New York Times* said the crowd called.

"We cannot allow the triumph of brutes," one man said.

The Turk's strength was called Herculean, but he was never the hero.

Not long after, in a rematch with a proper ring, the Turk lifted Roeber into the air and threw him first at one post then another until finally all four were broken, Roeber punched the Turk in the face, and the match was ended by the police. This time a draw.

YOU DON'T LIKE *my asking you questions, do you?*

*You're just doing your job.*

*Yes. But you don't like it.*

*It's not what I expected.*

*What did you expect?*

*Different kinds of questions.*

*What kind?*

*About my work. About where I'll live. About, I don't know, paying taxes, obeying the law.*

*We'll get to those.*

*Do you tell everybody these stories?*

*I tell everybody stories.*

*But not these stories.*

*No, not these stories. Do you think Roeber could have beaten Yusuf Ismail in a fair fight?*

*I think it was a fair fight. Why are you telling me these stories?*

*Roeber bent the rules, you might say.*

*Why are you telling me these stories?*

*You really think Roeber fought fair?*

———

*Do you really think Roeber fought fair?*

*Fair enough.*

*Do you think that's a particularly American way to win?*

*No.*

*Do you think Yusuf Ismail knew what was happening?*

*Yes.*

*So you think it was fixed? The Turk agreed to throw the fight? To throw Roeber off the mat? To put on a show?*

*I don't know. You're the one making this up, you tell me.*

*I'm not making it up.*

*Why did you tell me Roeber was a handsome man?*

*He was a handsome man. That's what people say of him. I didn't make that up.*

*But it's subjective, don't you think? How do you know what I find handsome?*

*Generally speaking, many people considered Roeber a handsome man.*

*But you told me that for a reason.*

*I'm telling you everything for a reason.*

*You're trying to get me to reveal something. This is some kind of weird game. A psychological test. That's it, isn't it? You are evaluating me on some kind of psychological test.*

*This isn't a test.*

*I'm going to call my lawyer. I don't believe this is legal.*

*Of course it's legal. I'm just doing my job, as you say.*

*Then ask me the proper questions.*

## The Fight at Cirque d'Hiver
**Paris, 1894**
**Four years before he died**
He was nervous with his hands all of the time. He opened and closed them, wiggled his fingers, he should have been a piano player with those fingers. All of the time, he moved his hands.

He spoke so frequently in pantomime that even when another Turkish fighter was on the bill, he often forgot to speak aloud. When he clapped his hands together it meant he was ready to fight. When he held his hands out in supplication it meant he did not understand. When he rubbed one hand on his stomach it meant either he was hungry or he was full. When he pointed his finger to his eye then stared hard at his manager it meant he didn't trust him, and he better watch himself. When he pounded his hand on his heart it meant he was grateful.

It was said to be the most horrific, the bloodiest, the most savage bout ever wrestled on a mat. Brutal. Brutes. Turk versus Turk. Yusuf Ismail versus Ibrahim Mahmout. Yusuf was bigger but Ibrahim was stronger, just as tall, and more muscular.

It was said only another Turk could challenge Yusuf, who, by then, had won all of his European bouts in a matter of minutes, most often in a matter of seconds.

They were to fight Turkish-style, no holds barred.

They approached without speaking, their faces unemotional— trancelike, some would say later.

The first time blood streamed from Ibrahim's nose, the referee stopped the fight to examine him. "It is nothing," Ibrahim said.

In the end, Ibrahim's nostrils were torn, his ribs broken, his arms turned in their sockets, and his clothes were streaked with his own blood. The Parisian women in the crowd wept at the sight of him. But he was the first wrestler in all of Europe to last longer than five minutes against the great Yusuf, the other, more terrible Turk.

Three times Tom Cannon, the referee, had tried to stop the fight, but neither man would release his hold, until finally Cannon, a fighter himself and no small man, beat at Yusuf with a stick. Yusuf paused long enough to glare at him, and Cannon retreated to a corner of the ring, as if he were the one conceding the match. A police inspector summoned six of the largest spectators he could see, and they approached Yusuf from two sides. Three to an arm they pulled at Yusuf, as if the only way to stop him wrestling was to split him in two. As they pulled, all six off-balance and leaning backward as if in a tug-of-war, the great fighter spun like an angry dervish so that all six men holding him lifted into the air. Ibrahim backed away suddenly, like a man just awakened. He stared down, confused, at the mat, which was covered in his blood.

"Would you like us to arrest him?" the police inspector asked Ibrahim. Ibrahim drew back, straightened, and with one hand resting on his damaged ribs, said, "But we were only wrestling."

*WHAT DO YOU THINK OF THAT?*
*I think it's nonsense.*
*Why?*
*Because it is, it's nonsense. The policemen, the great nobility of the savages, it's all nonsense.*
*So you think it's made up?*
___
*Do you think it's made up?*
___
*You don't want to answer?*
*Ask me the proper questions and I will answer.*

**The Fight at Kirkpinar**
**Turkey, 1887**
**Eleven years before he died**
It was nothing but an enormous empty field, really. No arena, no grandstands, no statues or plaques to memorialize the hun-

dreds of years of tournaments that had been held there already. But even empty, when the grass was no longer matted down in a hundred makeshift rings and the oil and sweat of the fighters had been absorbed into the earth, it had the feel of a battle-field. Men had wrestled there, the summer hunting grounds of the sultan, since 1690. Back then it was the sultan's renowned guard, the Janissaries, who had stripped down, greased each other with oil, fought for days, then celebrated for days more.

By the 1800s, the wrestlers wore ox-hide shorts down past their knees, and it was those that provided most of the holds. The only rule was that one man could not invade another's rectum with his fingers. They all kept their hair short so that it could not provide a hold. There was no cover from the sun, and the matches took place only feet apart, so that sometimes one pair of men tumbled into another pair's fight. In that case, all four would separate, step back, then begin again without argument or complaint. If one man got grass in his eye, it was his opponent who ran for water and a rag and then wiped at the afflicted area until it was clear.

Hundreds of men came to compete, and thousands more, men and women, came to watch. The field was surrounded by tents for sleeping, for eating, for drinking, for dancing. Before each fight, each pair of combatants would pray and then loosen their arms and then help oil each other—including their ox-hide shorts—a ritual as old as the tournament.

Yusuf did not look ahead to the end, when a champion would be named, nor did he watch any of the matches, some happening just a few feet from his own, nor did he participate in any of the surrounding festivities. He wrestled one match and then another and when he wasn't wrestling he entered a timeless state in which all he did was wait for his next match.

He was noticeable because of his size, and there was always a moment as he approached each new opponent when the opponent took him in all at once and then tried not to react. By the second day many of them knew Yusuf's name, though he was young and had never wrestled at Kirkpinar before. By the time he reached the championship match, everyone knew him by name. His opponent would be the most popular wrestler the empire had ever had, a wrestler who had won the tournament for each of the past twenty-six years, a record unmatchable now or then. Kel Aliço.

As Yusuf poured oil onto his hands to rub onto Kel Aliço's back, he noticed his hands trembling, and he clapped them together as if to wake them up. Kel Aliço smiled.

They wrestled five hours with only one fall.

At the end of the fifth hour, Kel Aliço leaned toward Yusuf and said, "I cannot beat you."

He stepped back and made a half bow to Yusuf, then a half bow to the spectators, who were first silent and then in an uproar. The renowned champion had named his successor. Yusuf was instantly beloved.

DO YOU THINK, in choosing to immigrate, the Turk made a mistake?

—

Do you think in choosing to immigrate he made a mistake?
He didn't immigrate, he went on tour.
Do you think in choosing to go on tour he made a mistake?

—

*He could have remained the Ottoman champion.*

*Yes, I get it.*

*A hero like Kel Aliço.*

———

*He could have spent his whole life in Turkey, never gotten on a boat.*

*I get it.*

*Do you think in choosing to go on tour he made a mistake?*

*He could have died anyway.*

*True.*

*I mean, he would have. Eventually. He would have died anyway. Just differently.*

*So do you think he made a mistake?*

———

*He was already a champion.*

———

*Do you think that should have been enough for him?*

———

WHEN THE TWO SHIPS HIT, there was a sound like the clash of swords.

When two men hit, there is the slap of skin, the slide of hands trying to find purchase on greased and sweaty skin, a reverberation of force that ripples first through their outer layers of flesh and then through their organs. Their collision displaces energy into their two bodies, and each tries to use that against the other. It becomes an energy they share.

There was a tremor through the two ships as well, but each passenger had to bear it on their own.

I imagine that before the collision, on the boat, Yusuf must have thought often of reaching home. He was ready to retire. But I imagine, too, that he was afraid. He had some money, he had a family to return to, but it was all unknown; he had spent his life wrestling, traveling. He was famous, of course, but he had daughters he barely knew and a wife who had grown accustomed to living without a husband. He had things to be ashamed of. He had never had much of a life outside of wrestling, so what would it be like to no longer have wrestling?

It would be nice to imagine that in the water he did not think of his fights with men but, rather, of how he used to train against nature, and how though he never defeated it, nature always made him stronger. How beautiful if he was able to remember his home with the cypress trees, the wind from the east, and the fields full of filberts and pistachios and chestnuts, later to be roasted in a fire.

As a boy Yusuf often flew into rages, but he burst into tears nearly as often.

As a boy he was terrified of quicksand, and in the end, the water held him, pulled him down, just as he had long ago imagined the earth could do.

It is said his bloated body washed up on a shore of the Azore Islands where it was found by a Catholic priest, who had him buried in the church garden.

His belt of gold was never found.

His family received nothing when he died.

*WHAT DO YOU THINK OF THAT?*

*Nothing.*

*It doesn't make you sad?*

*No.*

*I think you're lying to me.*

*Ask me the proper questions.*

*I just want you to reconsider. I don't think you should make any decisions now. Stay where you are. You don't have to decide now. We'll just hold off on the paperwork. You might be better off where you are, don't you think?*

*I want to speak to your supervisor.*

*I won't approve you, not yet. Not until you've thought about what we've talked about.*

*I want to speak to your supervisor. Or you'll be hearing from my lawyer.*

*Just go home and reconsider. Then, if you want to, you can try again.*

*This isn't right. It's not for you to decide.*

*But it is, isn't it?*

*Either you ask me the proper questions or I speak to your supervisor or I speak to a lawyer.*

——

——

*All right. If you insist. Though I think you are making a mistake.*

——

——

——

*All right then. Here we go. I'll stamp it. But you'll see.*

——

*You'll remember my words. I assure you, you will.*

# ICONOGRAPHY

$\ggg\!\!-\!\!-\!\!-\!\!-\!\!-\!\!-\!\!-\!\!-\!\!-\!\!-\!\!\longrightarrow$

Soon there will be a girl who will not eat. Some will call her the Turkish Girl; others, the Starving Girl.

Like most, I will read about her, then track her day to day in the news. I, like many, will find her beautiful, though I won't know why.

IT WILL HAPPEN, simply, like this:

One day she wakes feeling full, and so she skips breakfast, then lunch, then dinner, and she wakes the next day so hungry she still doesn't eat, the pain so exquisite that it feels true. It feels exactly like her.

But that truth is little known.

Most think she got the idea from the news, from the hundred and one Turks, including teenage girls, who died protesting the government's treatment of those imprisoned for their politics. Others think it was Gandhi. Or Thoreau, who she read for her freshman seminar at her American university, or Kafka in European Lit the next semester. Some blame websites, call it an eating disorder. Some call it misguided idealism, student politics overrunning common sense, the fault of a twenty-four-hour fast sponsored by the Students for a Sustainable Society (which she joined on her way to the dining hall one night). Actually, there is no evidence she participated in the fast, as it was an honor system kind of thing, and, in fact, she forgot to starve that day, which was weeks before her own fast, and that day, in fact, she ate not only three meals but shared a sausage pizza with her roommates around nine p.m., three hours before the fast, which she forgot to begin, was to end.

BEFORE SHE WILL BE the Starving Girl, she is not even the girl but merely *a* girl, an international student at an expensive American university, not terribly political, not terribly religious. Not even terribly Turkish.

FIRST SHE FASTS IN SILENCE. Nobody notices. Then they ask if she is losing weight. You look great, they say. And then, You look thin. And then, Do you want my ice cream, pasta, cereal bar, bagel, Diet Coke? And finally they call university administrators, who call her parents, who fly in, as soon as they can, from Ankara, where they run a hotel near the Atatürk mausoleum, which they are forced to leave in the hands of their assistant manager, who takes the opportunity to allow all of his distant relatives from the east to visit for free, with the result that one impressionable cousin removes her head scarf at the foot of Atatürk's statue, refuses to replace it despite the quiet insistence of her parents, and ends up leaving her family for good. The Starving Girl's parents would be affected by this story, by their implicit participation in the splitting of a family, but they, due to their own troubles, never hear it.

NEVER DOES THE STARVING GIRL think of herself as anything but hungry. It is the others who give her act drama, and meaning, which, in the end, she is happy to accept.

THE AMERICAN UNIVERSITY moves her to the student health center while they wait for her parents. Nobody, even she, is sure exactly how long it has been since she has eaten. At the health center, her professors, her roommates, her friends, and a number of strangers are brought in one at a time and then in groups. They ask her to eat. The president of the American university asks her to eat. Her roommates ask her to eat. The nurses ask her to eat. The president, the roommates, and the nurses together ask her to eat. What do we need to do to make you eat? they ask.

Change everything, she says.

It is the first thought that comes to her mind.

The next day the president of the American university brings in a boy who lived in a tree for nearly two years and who is also an alumnus, and he asks her to eat. You need to live so you can spread your message, the tree boy says. My death is my message, the Starving Girl says. My hunger is my message. She smiles a little smile as she says it. At least, so the alumnus tree boy will write in his memoir years later.

Can you be more specific? the president of the American university asks. About the message?

It is a very political university. They do not mind political actions as long as they have meaning and nobody is seriously hurt.

I hunger, the Starving Girl says.

For what?

For everything to be different.

The tree boy gets angry. Not everything should be different. Some things are really great. Some things need to stay exactly the same, he says.

The Starving Girl looks at him and again she smiles. It may be that she is too weak to speak; it may be that she has nothing to say. Or maybe she finds him funny. I wouldn't like to say.

BECAUSE OF THE VISITORS—the friends and strangers—most of campus hears about the Starving Girl, and so a reporter, who is also in the Starving Girl's European Lit class, in which they read Kafka, and who is from the university newspaper, comes to interview her.

What is it that you are trying to say? he asks.

She leans in closer to him, sliding along her bed, and looks into his face, but she does not answer.

Do you resent the contribution that food growers are making to global warming? he continues. Is it the pesticides? The cattle farts? The trucks and planes that move food millions of miles every day? The people's need to eat tomatoes all year long, as if summer is eternal?

Could you repeat the question? she says, and they both laugh.

But really, he says. Doesn't that stuff bother you?

Of course, she says, just above a whisper. Everything bothers me.

Is it the fattening of the poor? The fast-fooding of the nation? The Starbucking of the city? The drive-through, drive-by habit of eating that allows us to graze all day until our hearts explode with oversatiation and implode with alienation?

It's everything, she says.

That is where it really begins. STUDENT PROTESTS EVERY-THING is the headline to the article picked up by the *New York Times*.

THE STARVING GIRL'S PARENTS are temporarily detained when first the Turkish government and then the American take them in for questioning, one for leaving the country, the other for entering.

More reporters come, and at first she is just another ideal-istic teenager put into the spotlight before she has the skills to handle it. It is part of her initial charm. She quietly says things like: I'm not a role model. I'm not trying to change anybody's behavior. I'm doing this just for me. She was always soft-spoken and on the verge of thin. But then one day she stops talking, just as she had stopped eating, and becomes something more.

The students camp in front of the student health center at night and carry signs saying, "It's Everything," during the day. They would continue with their coursework—it's a good school after all, the students practiced multitaskers—but the faculty take a bus to Washington and camp in front of the White House, and so classes are canceled.

Soon there are articles speculating about the Starving Girl's love life, and reporters ask her opinion, which she does not offer, on many different world matters.

Bono comes to visit.

It all happens very quickly.

Soon the world is split between those who want to feed her, those who want to join her, and those who are afraid.

In Turkey, she becomes first a symbol of the East—the sacrificial martyr—and then a symbol of the West—the liberal protestor—and finally, yet one more point of interpretation and argument.

IN A MIDNIGHT VISIT, the president of the American university tells the Starving Girl how proud he is of her—this may be a real chance, he says, for not just the nation but the world to change—but the only way to keep this thing going is if she does not die and so won't she please eat. It would be their secret. The president is an exceptionally tall man, an advantage when speaking to crowds, but now he tries to round his shoulders in, to bend at the knees, to get closer to the Starving Girl. He crouches down by her bed, puts his hand on hers, and has to resist pulling it away when he feels how cold her fingers are.

No secrets, she says, speaking for the first time in days. But I will take some water.

For just a moment the president of the American university wants to call her a stupid bitch, even though he is not the kind of person to think, let alone say, such a thing. Look what this is doing to me, he thinks. He straightens in a bolt, yanks his hand out of hers when her fingers tangle with his, and leaves without remembering to bring her water.

Inside the Starving Girl's mouth, the soft palate, the uvula, the tonsils, the anterior and posterior pillars are all dry. The nurses have been teaching her anatomy, in the hopes that it will connect her to her body. And in some sense it has. Now when she is bored she reads herself like a textbook, cataloging her parts and how they feel.

A DOCTOR WHO IS FAMOUS for talking on television, and who happens to be Turkish, comes in and explains what will happen to her body if she continues to refuse food: the ache, the muscles burning as they deteriorate, constricting in on themselves, the disintegration of her organs, the blackening of her sight, the elimination of her hearing, the bleeding under her skin.

I can live with that, she says, her voice a quiet croak. She is disappointed when the doctor does not deliver the obvious comeback: Not for long you can't.

In fact, with each day the sensations of her body are a mystery, awe-inspiring in their intensity. The Turks were among the first to infect a person with a disease in order to prevent it. They knew that sometimes you had to be sick in order to live. The Starving Girl does not know this intellectually, but in her body she does. She thinks, in her long dying, that she is completely alive. And strangely happy.

FINALLY THE STARVING GIRL's parents arrive, and first, like the university, refuse to force her to eat. They take her from the student health center into their room at the local hotel and let her lie in bed and watch cable television. They have heard watching television leads to eating. Their daughter has changed since coming to America; they think maybe they need to treat her like an American. But they do not know that the Starving Girl is watching only the shifting lights on the screen as if they are an unending Fourth of July display.

Sometimes she drinks water with sugar from the hotel's in-room coffee station. She can still stand and walk to the bathroom if she takes her time.

When she wakes at night with her mother beside her and her father on the cot the hotel rolled into the room and unfolded like a hospital bed, the Starving Girl thinks of what will happen when she dies. Her mother will wash her body alone, not even looking at it as she works her hands and washcloth underneath the sheet that shrouds the body, no longer recognizable by touch. For the Starving Girl it is a beautiful memory.

For years her cheeks held a roundness that was not matched by any other part of her body. When she was a young girl, her mother would cup her fat cheeks and say, Baby. Sometimes she did it even when the girl was a teenager. Sometimes her father did it. Baby, they would say.

At first her parents do nothing but suggest room service, chocolate from the minibar, pretzels from the vending machine on the third floor. Then they bring in *mantı* and *lahmacun,* the Starving Girl's former favorite foods, from the closest Turkish restaurant, which is more than fifty miles away. The restaurant's chef, when he hears who the customer is, volunteers to travel to the hotel and cook fresh in their kitchen, but her parents say there is no reason to come; she will not eat. She is no longer hungry.

AND HOW WOULD YOU describe hunger? We live as if we know what we want, as if we are capable of deciphering the signals our bodies send us, but what if we are wrong? I may say hunger feels like illness, but how can I know how it felt to her? Or what if hunger is an illness that eating covers but doesn't cure? Could eating be one more drug that masks the disease?

MOST OF THE TIME, she is in a state between fantasizing and dreaming. Newspaper headlines float in front of her, captioning a future in which hundreds, then thousands of students join her fast, followed by the elderly, then the overworked, the immigrants, the stay-at-home parents, their toddlers, the teachers, the small business owners, the used-book sellers, the hedge fund brokers, the CEOs, residents of the West, of the South, of the East, until finally no one is eating. It is a hunger strike so large that everything changes, and for at least a year ours is a world in which everyone helps each other and the worst things that happen are the kinds of arguments you have when you are tired but that can be solved when you are rested again.

It is not a future she invents; she believes it is the future come to her.

And maybe it is.

WHAT IS THE WORD, she asks her mother in a whisper. Her mother waits. The Starving Girl points a finger into her upper arm, like she is shooting herself. Inoculation, her mother says, and the girl nods. I am the inoculation, she says. I am the little bit of sickness that stops the disease, she says. Her mother shakes her head, but her daughter has already closed her eyes. I am the spotlight, the Starving Girl says with her eyes closed, and it is as if she has shut them against her own bright light.

WHEN FINALLY THE Starving Girl cannot rise without help and she wets the bed, then lies without comment on the damp sheets until her mother slides in next to her and says, What's this, only then do her parents call the president of the American university again. They do not know who else to ask for help. The president suggests an eating disorder clinic that will take the girl, lock her in, feed her one way or another. If it is a choice between saving the world and saving his student, he will save his student, he tells the administrative assistant who is in the room when he takes the call. The president offers to arrange a ride to the clinic. The Starving Girl's mother does not want to say yes, she is ashamed of her inability to care for her own daughter, but she does say yes, as does the girl's father. What else could they do? They do not want to be parents to a martyr; it is not an honor they would choose.

So that afternoon, just as the first of a convention's worth of pharmaceutical sales representatives is checking in at the front desk, the Starving Girl's father carries her through the halls of the local hotel, down the elevator, and staggering through the lobby, into the waiting car arranged by the president.

She is not light; she is heavy.

The pharmaceutical sales representative and all those in the hotel lobby that day are the last to admit to seeing her or her family. Later they each comment on how the father seemed as if he might fall, and how he refused their help, which in truth they did not offer.

THERE WILL BE DISPUTE over what happens next.

Some say the Starving Girl is cured by the clinic, unbrainwashed or brainwashed, depending on your point of view, so that she eats and maybe forgets, too, her hunger. She returns to the American university under a different name and graduates and returns to Turkey, or she returns to the American university under a different name and graduates and stays in the U.S. Or she returns to Turkey under a different name without graduating. Or she stays in the U.S. under a different name without graduating. In any case, she blends back in with the rest of us.

But some say the car she is riding in is intercepted by the Students for a Sustainable Society who held the first twenty-four-hour fast, and who have been holding a sympathy strike of their own, though they alternate days of not eating, as death is not part of the sustainable message, and the Students for a Sustainable Society take the Starving Girl to an undisclosed location, where they offer her a choice: eat or don't. We don't mind either way, they say. Some say given this freedom, the Starving Girl eats. Some say she doesn't. Some say her beauty and her hunger inspire all of the Students for a Sustainable Society who took her to the undisclosed location to stop eating and they all die, unseen and unfound, forever. Others say the Students and the girl start a revolution so underground that few people even know the effects of their actions, which are many.

Some say she moves to Canada.

Some make jokes.

Others say other things.


ONE STORY IS THIS:

The car does not take her to an eating disorder clinic. It takes her to a secret location set up by the government underneath another secret location, where her parents are immediately disappeared. They last see their daughter with her eyes closed and her head tilted against the window of the limo, a small smudge of fog on the glass where her breath hits it, the only sign that she is still alive. They are taken from the car, forcibly in the case of her father, by two men who are neither tall nor short, large nor small, dark nor light, wearing clothes that are instantly forgotten and expressions that are cold in that they are blank. The men take the Starving Girl's parents to another car, a black sport-utility vehicle, and that is the last that is known of them, though years later it is believed by many that an elderly woman who surfaces at a Tibetan monastery with no memories of her past is actually the Starving Girl's mother.

The Starving Girl, who cannot anymore remember if she is a person, is placed underground in a room that looks like a hospital room but is not. The government keeps her alive while they decide whether or not they would prefer her to die. There she floats, a body adrift without its mind, and a mind adrift without its body, for several days, until the doctor who is assigned to care for her, a man who has never married and never had children but has always longed for both marriage and children, and who is believed to be working for the government but isn't, brings in a select group of journalists, celebrities, and intellectuals, all of whom he was once a doctor for, to meet her during the night.

Her skin is tight in places, sagging in others. Her bones show. Her hair is mostly gone. Her fingers twitch. And she smells.

I am the only one to touch her. I kneel next to her bed, and encircle her wrist with my thumb and forefinger. She does not move.

"What do you want?" I ask loud enough for the others, clumped together across the room, to hear.

Some believe she does not answer. Others believe she says, "Get up." Others insist it is "Give up."

I know what she said. But I will not tell you. This is your story, not mine.

The doctor asks the select group of journalists, celebrities, and intellectuals what he should do. Should I save her? he asks. Or do I maintain my cover and see what else the government gets up to?

The group is silent, thinking the same thing, until finally one, the oldest and most famous, a woman with a sheath of bright white hair that she has pulled back in a slick ponytail, says it: You should let her die.

The others look to me, as if having touched her, I have some special say. My fingers tingle where they touched her wrist. Maybe it is her action that allows our inaction. Maybe her action was so large it left no room for ours.

Remember: an absence of action is an action, just as an absence of belief is a belief.

Remember: it is easy to love and hate her, both. To believe "get up" and "give up" are simultaneously sensible options.

And so she dies.

This is the kind of thing that can happen when you give up your body. Others do what they want with it. And your body is more of you than you perhaps imagined—with her body went her intent, her words, her self.

She's mine now. And yours, too.

BUT THAT IS NOT the only way. Here is another:

At the eating disorder clinic, where she is delivered without incident, the Starving Girl meets many girls and older women, too. We don't talk much. Meals—when so many others socialize—are too fraught for us. Many of the girls eat in their rooms with only a counselor present. Even when we are together in the dining room, it's an unspoken rule that nobody speaks. Talk is usually in the shared bathrooms or late at night with our roommates, and mostly that is the whispered swapping of strategies for when we are clear of this place.

We did not know she was coming, but when she arrived it was obvious she was special. There were photographers outside—we could see them from the windows. And the staff whispered together. Finally somebody saw her, recognized her from the news. She was for us a hero. She hid her disease in plain sight, under the guise of politics.

At first she was in the medical ward. They called her by a different name, but we knew it was her. We decided to strike, too. Just as soon as we were on the outside. She was an inspiration. Even when she told us not to, when we watched her gain weight, when we watched her family visit and leave smiling and finally one day leave with her, walking on her own, we all knew we would strike. She could have said anything and it wouldn't have stopped us. She had given us the idea, created the cause, and each of us waited, eating our half portions, gaining our single digits, eating just enough, saying just the right things to move to our freedom. She ate, but she left the rest of us hungry. And you have to understand, hunger for us was proof that we were alive. Our future strike glowed inside each of us, something to live for, even if it would kill us. I do not exaggerate. Inside of us, she glowed.

REALLY, THERE ARE SO MANY ways this story could end. Remember, it has not happened yet. But here is my last:

I help the Starving Girl and her parents into the car, then slide in behind the wheel. Her mother sits in front, while she and her father sit in the back.

"Please," her father says as he straps on first her seat belt and then his own, and the Starving Girl looks at him gently.

"Without you, I would not be able to live," he says.

He is not one to beg.

She pauses. Then finally she says, "Okay."

And instead of saving the world, she saves him.

# LITTLE SISTER AND EMINEH

>>> ————————————————————>

> You sit here for days saying, "This is strange business."
> You are the strange business.
>
> —RUMI

There was John Alden's Bible, a piece of Plymouth Rock, Myles Standish's pipe, Aaron Burr's calling card, and a weather report written in the hand of George Washington. There was the gun that fired the first shot of the Civil War, and the gun that fired the last. There was a four-inch armadillo from the Argentine and the first photograph of the moon. An eight-foot elephant tusk and a set of ivory napkin rings. A Zulu xylophone and the clothes of a Russian priest. A collection of wax fruit, colored sketches of poisonous and edible fungi, and a machine that planted trees. The whole thing was built on a swamp and included a wooded island with a Japanese garden and an acre of roses.

There were nearly six thousand speeches given. There was the first Ferris wheel. A Liberty Bell made of oranges, grapefruits, and lemons, a twenty-two-thousand-pound wheel of cheese, and a map of the United States made of pickles. There was the most powerful searchlight in the world, soldiers' skulls by the thousands, certain portions of John Wilkes Booth, and two rifle balls that hit each other midair during the Battle of Gettysburg, each flattened on one side by the impact.

It was a city of its own that used three times the electricity of Chicago's downtown. More than eighteen thousand tons of iron and steel and seventy-five million feet of wooden boards went into its construction. Forty-seven states and territories and fifty-one countries sent displays. It took two years to build, which wasn't much, considering. Early attendance was sparse; but in the end more than twenty-seven million people came, including Annie Oakley, Harry Houdini, Nikola Tesla, Scott Joplin, Clarence Darrow, Woodrow Wilson, Teddy Roosevelt, Susan B. Anthony, Theodore Dreiser, L. Frank Baum, and Helen Keller.

Mark Twain tried but took ill in his hotel.

There were exhibits of collars and cuffs, of trunks, of paper, of stoves, of hardware for saddles, of wire, of sewing machines, of door screens, Vaseline, and cork. There was a Brooklyn Bridge built of soap. A stuffed polar bear carrying a flag. A Windsor Castle built of soap. A seventy-six-foot Viking ship. A Statue of Liberty built of soap. Hans Christian Andersen's desk and his umbrella. Beethoven's grand piano. Haydn's grand piano. Mozart's spinet. The first telegram. A handwritten manuscript of *Jane Eyre*. An Indian elephant built of walnuts. A windmill built of salt. A model of the U.S. Treasury Building built of souvenir coins. A castle built of tobacco and a moonshiner's cabin.

There was an anteater from British Guiana and cereal from New South Wales. Lafayette's sword, needlework done by the queen of England, Edison's Kinetoscope, Edison's phonograph, and Edison's electric tower, eighty-two feet tall and lit by thousands of miniature lamps. There was the largest load of logs ever drawn by one team and a chocolate Venus de Milo. There was a dungeon, a torture chamber, and the first electric chair. Also a knight on horseback made of prunes.

There was a logger's camp, an Indian school, a lighthouse, a weather bureau, a fisherman's camp, a military hospital, and a Japanese teahouse. There were twenty-four Laplanders, their dogs, and their reindeer (who died one by one when the heat of summer came). There was a German village, an East Indian village, an American Indian village, a panorama of the Bernese Alps, a Chinese village, an Austrian village, a panorama of the volcano Kilauea, a Dahomey village, a Dutch settlement, a Moorish palace, a Cairo street, the Wild East Show, a Japanese bazaar, an Irish village, an Eskimo village, a French café, the Hagenbeck Animal Show, the California Ostrich Farm, a tethered balloon, and the sixty-five residents of the Turkish Village, not all technically Turks.

They didn't know it, but the villages were meant to be an evolutionary chart running from savage to civilized.

They lived there for over six months—along the Midway

Plaisance, an arm of the World's Columbian Exposition of 1893, known as the Chicago World's Fair—in between the panorama of the Alps and the Moorish Palace, across from the German Village and the Dutch Settlement, under the shadow of the Ferris wheel.

They were a family of sorts. Men, women, and children from cities all over the East: Jerusalem, Bethlehem, Nazareth, Damascus, Beirut, Lebanon, Aleppo, Smyrna, and Constantinople. They had arrived a month before the fair began, after a steamer trip from Constantinople to New York, and a train trip from New York to Chicago. And at the end of the fair, they would, with one exception, make the trip in reverse, the train from Chicago to New York, the steamer from New York to Constantinople, where they would again work in theaters and bazaars and restaurants until the next opportunity arose to perform their part of the world in another.

Inside the village, there were shops, restaurants, a Persian tent that was a hundred and sixty years old, thirteen houses, and a mosque. There were camels, Bedouins, Arabian horses, swordplay, and mock battles. There was a pavilion with sweet Turkish drinks and a café with Turkish coffee. The most popular exhibit was a bed made of silver, which weighed three thousand pounds and belonged to a sultan's daughter. There were actors and acrobats, dancing girls and weavers, swordsmen and salesmen, sedan-chair carriers and even fake Turkish beggars, a handful of boys dressed in rags, as well as one girl dressed as a boy dressed in rags. That was Little Sister.

When it was discovered that Little Sister was not a boy— she was not before then called Little Sister, of course—she was sent to share a bed with Emineh, who was but fifteen and whose task it was to kneel before a loom in the bazaar weaving the same wool carpet each day. She had been told to pick out her work each night so that she would never run out of wool; but she could not bear to always go back to the same beginning, so that each day the rug was a little larger, though not enough for anyone to notice (until one day they did).

At her loom, Emineh was quiet, though she had memories of being a much louder girl. Sometimes at her loom, she thought she was no longer Emineh but instead was her own mother, transported from the past to the present, eight years after dying. Emineh was quietest then, because she did not know what her mother would say.

Life on the Midway resembled a series of poses rather than a sequence of actions. The villagers sat for newspaper photographers and for amateur photographers, they sat for sketches and for watercolorists. They waited for customers, they waited on customers. They acted their lives in a manner in which they had never lived. They spoke English to the fairgoers but not to each other, so that private words could be spoken in public. And Emineh learned secrets she did not wish to know. It was easy for the others to forget she was there, behind the loom, silently weaving, pretty as a picture.

There were at least three swordsmen in love with her.

It was hard to remember that Emineh was fifteen. Everyone seemed to forget, including her.

She was small, but her eyes were large, and her hair—it was like an element of its own—a shimmering golden brown, and soft. People were always reaching out to touch her hair, and she was always turning away from them, so that their fingers skimmed just alongside its waves. Men had been known to pocket single strands they found on the floor. Women had been known to pull strands from her pillow and wrap them around their wrists as good-luck charms.

At night, Emineh did not mind sharing her bed with Little Sister, though it was the smallest of all the beds, because she was so often cold, even in summer, and she found Little Sister worked better than a hot-water bottle (not as wet) or a hot brick (which inevitably grew cool as the night wore on). Plus, Emineh saw in the little orphan girl someone whose past and future both seemed so desolate that Emineh hoped something could be done to improve her present.

Little Sister was only seven. And while she was allowed to keep her position as a fake beggar boy, she was told that at the end of the fair she would be returned to her orphanage unless some other, more suitable role could be found for her. The boys had been taken from the orphanage with the expectation that they would grow up to become actors or acrobats or swordsmen for future concessions. But Little Sister did not look likely to become a dancing girl and so far was known only for her extraordinary ability to remain quiet for great lengths of time.

Though she often whispered in the night to Emineh.

What Little Sister was saying, Emineh could never tell, but the fifteen-year-old learned to fall asleep to the murmuring voice of the seven-year-old. Often she heard it in her dreams. Often she woke with Little Sister's hand nested in her hair, and Little Sister's mouth at her ear.

Fair days began early and lasted late, but at the end there

was always a time when the gates had closed, and the strag-
glers had been expelled, and the villagers had their village to
themselves. Some would stagger to bed, but many would sit
together in the café, where they would eat their first meal of
the day, a distorted Ramadan in which they fasted not for faith
but because they were too busy working.

Mother Zeyno would be the one to start.

Once there was and once there wasn't.

Folktales, family tales, tales of the fair.

Little Sister would sit on the floor, in a corner of the room
closest to the door. The other beggar boys were in bed already,
tucked in after their evening training with horses and swords,
but nobody seemed to care enough about Little Sister to send
her to bed. One night Emineh sat down on the floor beside her,
and from then on they sat together, until the hour came when
Emineh could stay awake no longer and she would lead Little
Sister off to sleep. Emineh always tried to stay awake until
Mehmet Bey and Ahmet Bey, who carried fairgoers around the
grounds in a glassed-in sedan chair, had told their tale; it was
always her favorite. Besides, she liked how they were kind to
Little Sister, letting her sit in their chair whenever they were
not engaged.

*Once there was and once there wasn't, in the time when genies were
jinn and camels were couriers:*

*Mehmet Bey and Ahmet Bey returned to their sedan chair one
morning to find a baby sleeping inside. They carried the baby to and
fro across the fair, asking if anyone knew to whom it belonged. Finally
a guardsmen told them to take the baby to the Children's Building,
where there was a lost and found for just such things. But there the*

*woman in charge of the nursery looked at how well the baby slept
inside their sedan chair and handed them the squalling baby that was
in her own arms. "Come back when it's asleep," she said. And so Ahmet
Bey and Mehmet Bey spent an entire day walking crying babies across
the fair until they slept. The delighted nurse paid them two dollars
from her own pocketbook and asked them to come back the next day,
but the sound of crying haunted their ears all night, and when they
finally did sleep they dreamt only of constant walking, so they swore
from then on to avoid the Children's Building entirely, which they did.*

The villagers slept in two dormitories, men on the second
floor, women on the third. (Sometimes the creak of stairs
could be heard; the only way to privacy was for the man to
go up while the woman went down, so that they met in the
middle.) The women's dormitory consisted of a room with
ten beds shoved so close together that one had to crawl over
nine beds to get to the last. Emineh and Little Sister's bed
was closest to the door, which meant they never had to climb
over anyone else, but everyone else had to climb over them. At
night, when they were not yet asleep, the bodies passing over
them made them laugh; in the morning, when Mother Zeyno
woke early to pray and to urinate, it was not so funny.

Especially because Mother Zeyno liked to scold, especially
to scold Little Sister.

Little Sister was quiet, but she was often in the center of
things. "Why do you stand there?" Mother Zeyno would shout
at her. And Emineh would gesture Little Sister to her side and
hold her there. She had tried to teach Little Sister to weave,
but the girl was unwilling to learn. She would not even watch
Emineh's hands while she was instructed. "I don't blame you,"

Emineh said finally, quietly. "I would rather own a carpet than weave one."

But Emineh found she could distract Little Sister if she showed her the patterns she wove.

This is a woman with her hands on her hips; she is there to protect all children.

This is a purple hyacinth, which conveys melancholy.

This is a pink hyacinth, which conveys happiness.

This is a white hyacinth, which conveys loyalty.

This is an eagle, which can look straight into the sun.

And this, this figure here, is me.

And this, this figure here, is you.

And when Mother Zeyno was distracted, Emineh would send Little Sister on an errand she knew would never be filled. Little Sister was often sent places where she never arrived.

During the days, Little Sister could usually be found watching the Laplanders' bear, or the ostriches at the ostrich farm, or the swordsman who had trained his horse to pick up a sword from the ground with its teeth. As the weeks went on, Little Sister could usually be found holding the Arab's monkey or helping him train his performing goat. Or curled up in the shade with the Laplanders' dogs.

Sometimes she could be found following the Hagenbeck bears across their tightrope.

Each evening she curled against Emineh's side and nested her hand in Emineh's hair, as they listened to the others tell their tales.

*Once there was and once there wasn't, in the time when genies were jinn and camels were couriers:*

*An elderly British man fell in step alongside Mehmet Bey and Ahmet Bey as they carried his daughter, a solid woman of middle age, in their sedan chair. "I have heard the Orientals have a weakness to their legs," the old man said to one or the other or neither of them. "That is why they are so often seen sitting or lying down. In your case," he continued, turning first to Mehmet Bey and then to Ahmet Bey, "this does not appear to be true." "Perhaps," Mehmet Bey said. "Perhaps not," Ahmet Bey said as he pretended to buckle at the knees and the British man's daughter let out a small scream as the back end of the closed-in sedan chair dipped down and her whole self tilted backward with the bend of Ahmet Bey's legs. There was quiet for a moment as the British man stood staring and astonished, and then came a call from inside the chair: "Please. If you would. Do it again."*

At night, Little Sister whispered and Emineh dreamt that her heart took the shape of a leaping gazelle.

The villagers' nights always held a residue of their days.

The mind's ear remembered the booming of the Austrian brass band. The mind's eye remembered the reflection of the electric spotlights on the man-made lake. Across the dark they heard echoes of the Javanese flute players, the Dahomey drums, the bark of the Laplander dogs, and the cry of the Eskimo baby, who had been born three days after the fair began and died six days later.

Little Sister became a comfort Emineh had not known she needed.

At night, Little Sister whispered and Emineh dreamt that her heart took the shape of a blackbird's shadow.

Emineh had brothers and sisters but they'd never lived to be more than babies.

Six weeks after the fair began, the much-delayed Ferris wheel finally made its first turn and there was the sound of metal bearing down on metal, then the sound of loose bolts and lost buttons clattering down, then the sound of glass swaying in the air, and the sound of a thousand necks craning upward to follow the sound.

Little Sister lay down on the ground to look up at it.

The operators learned to leave her be.

When one of the swordsmen slipped into the women's dormitory to kiss Emineh while she was sleeping, it was Little Sister's stare that sent him away unfulfilled.

The same swordsman came to Emineh while she was weaving and offered to make her his wife.

"You have a wife in Aleppo," she said without looking up, "I heard you say so."

"It's true," he said. "I miss her terribly."

Emineh did not reply, but he did not leave.

Finally she said, "You have spent too much time among peacocks and nightingales."

Her voice was as sharp as the tip of a sultan's dagger the night before battle.

"And you have spent too much time among wolves," he said.

Perhaps he was right. Emineh had always wished to have the soft voice of the nightingale. But she never did.

"May I just . . ." and the swordsman reached out toward Emineh's hair.

"No," she said as she turned her head.

Little Sister whispered and Emineh dreamt that her heart took the shape of a wild thorn.

Each day, Emineh watched the American girls who came in to watch her weave. They never stayed long.

Which one of them was fifteen, she wondered.

Emineh was born to a carpet weaver and a carpet seller, but they had been destined to die young and when opportunity arose, Emineh followed it, first to Constantinople then to Chicago. She did not plan to return with the others; she would stay in America, somehow. Though that really was the extent of her plan.

Emineh tried to imagine taking Little Sister with her. But she couldn't.

One day, Emineh heard Mother Zeyno tell a customer about her dead sons.

On another she heard Mother Zeyno tell a customer about her dead daughters.

"Mother Zeyno," she said. "Did you really have children?"

"Yes," Mother Zeyno said, and she didn't say any more.

*Once there was and once there wasn't, in the time when genies were jinn and camels were couriers:*

*Ahmet Bey and Mehmet Bey had carried the last of their evening customers and so they rested their sedan chair beside the grand fountain and sat down inside their chair to rest their tired legs. From inside they could see the few remaining fairgoers pointing at the fountain's waters.*

*"What do you think is in there?" Ahmet Bey asked.*

*"A drowned person," Mehmet Bey answered.*

*"Surely then someone would get in a boat and retrieve the body," Ahmet Bey answered.*

*"If you are so curious, go look for yourself," Mehmet Bey said.*

*"I will," Ahmet Bey said.*

*Mehmet Bey watched Ahmet Bey exit the chair, walk to the foun-*
*tain, and then follow the pointing fingers of a young man and woman*
*he had approached. Ahmet Bey nodded, walked back to the sedan*
*chair, and settled himself inside with a laugh.*

*"What's so funny?" Mehmet Bey asked.*

*"They are looking at the moon in the water," Ahmet Bey said.*

*"Why is that funny?" Mehmet Bey asked.*

*"Because they do not seem to know the real thing is right above*
*them," Ahmet Bey answered.*

Little Sister whispered and Emineh dreamt that her heart
took the shape of an open tulip.

Emineh wove her carpet during the day and unwove it at
night under the strict supervision of Mother Zeyno, who had
noticed its increasing size.

Each day she wove symbols other than the day before, so
that the carpet grew dense with meaning. Only Little Sister
saw each image, including the ones that were no longer visible.

This is a phoenix, which is burned to ash and reborn.

This is a dragon, which conveys strength.

This is the Tree of Life with birds on its branches, to depict
the life that one day will fly away.

And this is my name written in script.

And this is your name written in script.

On the day when the Eskimos took off their furs and refused
to put them back on, the dancing girls found the furs in a pile
and wrapped each other tight and refused to unwind.

And on the ninth of July, the wind bore down and the tethered balloon lifted up, too high, too hard, and everyone looked

to see one man still holding his rope as the other workers screamed because they knew well there was a time when it was safe to let go and a time when it wasn't, and as the man's feet floated up from the ground and his arms strained in their sockets, he had entered the time when it wasn't. He fell much faster than he'd floated. Little Sister saw him and stared.

And on the tenth of July, when the Cold Storage Building caught fire, Little Sister saw only the smoke and the shadows of the firefighters as they took flight. A fire without flame. She cried.

The next day she stole ten cents from the cashbox and took her first ride on the Ferris wheel.

"Little Sister, you can't," Emineh said. "What if they caught you?"

That night Little Sister whispered and Emineh dreamt that her heart took the shape of the scimitar.

The next day Little Sister stole twenty cents from the cashbox and rode the Ferris wheel twice.

"I won't be able to protect you," Emineh said. "Do you want to go back to the orphanage?"

The next day Little Sister stole thirty cents from the cashbox and rode the Ferris wheel three times.

*Once there was and once there wasn't, in the time when genies were jinn and camels were couriers, in that time there was a thief who thought she could not be caught.*

Mother Zeyno was the one to tell that story. Of course.

"I would like to tell a story," Emineh said and everyone turned to her, surprised.

She tried to make the nightingale's sound, but her voice came out as sharp as the cold on the top of the eastern mountains.

*Once there was and once there wasn't, in the time when genies were jinn and camels were couriers, during that time there was a baby bird who broke its wing and so could not make the winter migration to warmer air. And so the baby bird's mother went first to the oak tree to ask if it would shelter her baby bird in winter, but the oak tree said no. And then she asked the walnut tree. And the olive tree. And every tree she could find, but they all said no. Until finally she asked the pine. And the pine made a nest among its needles for the baby bird, and all winter long, it kept the baby bird warm and safe by not dropping its needles. And ever since that winter, the pine tree has never shed its needles.*

"It would have been kinder to let the bird die," Mother Zeyno said. "It probably grew up weak and coddled and couldn't take care of itself."

"I think that's very cruel," Emineh said.

"Then you take care of the baby bird," Mother Zeyno said, and the others all laughed.

The next day Little Sister put her hand in the cashbox but Emineh took it out. She pressed her wool-roughened fingertips against Little Sister's soft palm. "For me," Emineh said, "stop."

Little Sister climbed instead to the top of the Manufactures Building and spent each day looking down.

"Where were you today?" Mother Zeyno would ask and someone else would answer: "I saw her at the swimming competition." "I saw her on the Wooded Island." "I saw her on the battleship."

And so Emineh told another story, this one in a voice as sharp as the knife that scraped the sheep's wool from their backs.

*Once there was and once there wasn't, in the time when genies were jinn and camels were couriers, during that time there was a girl who could appear in more than one place at one time.*

"What's the point?" Mother Zeyno said. "Who cares if you can be in two places at once if you aren't any good in either?"

And the next night, in a voice as sharp as the edge of a soldier's sword:

*Once there was and once there wasn't.*

*A girl who could float from the ground.*

"At least she'd be out of the way," Mother Zeyno said. "You could sweep under her feet."

And the next, in a voice as sharp as the eagle's claw dipped in the blood of its prey:

*Once there was and once there wasn't.*

*A girl who could tell a horse to run backward.*

Too bad the horse didn't run backward right over the girl who taught him such a useless trick.

And the next, in a voice as sharp as the petalless rose:

*A girl who could travel to Mecca and back in the time it took a spilled vase to empty of water.*

Too bad the Prophet didn't keep her there.

Too bad too bad too bad.

Emineh told her last story lying in bed with all of the other women lined up in their beds next to her and Little Sister tight in her arms.

*Once there was a girl who could make you dream.*

Emineh's voice glowed like the golden moon as Mother

Zeyno had seen it once, fat and full, over the mountains of her parents' village when she was no more than a girl.

*She could turn your heart into a shifting cloud. She could give you the strength to love all that was inside of you, which was everything.*

And when the story was over, Mother Zeyno said only, "I wish people would be quiet so an old woman could sleep."

That night, Little Sister whispered and Emineh dreamt that her heart took the shape of the world, and in the center of that world, inside of it, was Little Sister, inside of her.

The next morning Emineh was gone. Next to Little Sister in bed was the completed wool carpet rolled tight. When Little Sister unrolled the carpet and lay down on top of it and stretched out her fingertips to toy with the little tassels Emineh had knotted all along the carpet's edge, and then ran her finger over the pink hyacinth, the purple hyacinth, and the white, Little Sister felt her heart take the shape of Emineh's heart.

What happened to Emineh nobody would ever know. Probably she struggled, probably she was sorry. Probably she died.

"Sleep with me, child," Mother Zeyno said the next night, and Little Sister did, though they each could have, should they have wanted, had a bed entirely to themselves.

# MYSTERIES OF THE
# MOUNTAIN SOUTH

》》》———————————————————————→

"I like to talk about it," Edie's grandmother said.

"Death?" Edie said.

"Yeah," her grandmother said. "It makes me feel better."

IN MAY, EDIE HAD a job offer and a plan to follow the mass migration of her fellow coders west after their college graduation. She and her friends—absent Edie's unexpectedly-ex-boyfriend—would live in packs, turn large Victorians into something like their college co-op, ride company shuttles to work, and earn obscene amounts for obscene hours, doing work they didn't so much love as crave.

But then Edie's father said her grandmother would have to move into assisted living because: what else could she do? Edie's father lived in a studio apartment. His two brothers were cash-rich but time-poor. Edie's younger sister was only thirteen. And you couldn't ask the wife you'd divorced to take in your mother, could you? Maybe, but probably you shouldn't.

So in June, Edie drove south with some suitcases in her trunk, a company-sponsored drone in the backseat, and her newly rescued seven-year-old dog, Trixie Belden, in the seat beside her. Trixie was Edie's graduation present to herself because Edie had

always

always

always

wanted a dog.

Their drive to the hills of southwestern Virginia had taken only a long morning but had crossed, in what Edie couldn't help but think of as a time-traveler way, deeply into rural life. As if plain living were a thing of the past! As if excess belonged only to the present.

Mrs. Coxe's house was one story but spread wide, with a porch on three sides, potted plants all around, a weedy lawn in the front, and an overgrown vegetable patch on the porchless side. Edie stumbled out of the car, her legs stiff with driving, and Trixie followed. At first, the dog shuffled around gingerly, dysplasia starting in one hip, but soon her ears perked and her nose quivered, and she sniffed in a widening circle. Edie stepped onto her grandmother's porch, knocked, then turned to call Trixie, only to find she had disappeared.

Trixie Belden: a dog with a past. A bicolored border collie with a rough double coat. A dog always looking for the thing that was lost, the thing she could recall only with her senses, a shape here, a smell there, a taste of cherry lip gloss from a kiss on the lips: her former owner, a once-fourteen-year-old named Madeline who loved nothing more in the world than Trixie (née Emily Dickinson), the dog who'd disappeared from her backyard one afternoon in a forever cold case—gate still closed, doors still locked.

IT WAS MORE THAN an hour after Edie's initial arrival that she and her grandmother finally hugged hello. Their first greeting had been a strange, rushed thing in which Edie stammered out, "I have to go after my dog," then dashed off the porch without even looking her grandmother in the face, not even making entirely sure that the woman who'd opened the door was her grandmother. Anyway, the second time, they held each other tight, their first acknowledgment of Mrs. Coxe's terrible circumstances.

"I'm sorry, Grandma," Edie said, into Mrs. Coxe's ear.

"Fuck you and your pity," Mrs. Coxe whispered back, but she didn't let go.

THREE HUNDRED MILLION years ago the Appalachian Mountains were twenty thousand feet higher. Enormous ferns and tiny salamanders dominated. More recently, there were wild turkeys, panthers, bears, wolves, woodland bison, a hundred ravens and vultures and eagles watching over a single kill. Sometimes there were wolf traps and sometimes children torn to pieces. But by 2015, there were mostly squirrels and woodpeckers, a farm here and there, a golf course on one reclaimed mountaintop, a prison on another, gated communities in the valleys, stills turned to museums in the hollows, the occasional marijuana field or worse, but also amphitheaters, craft shows, music festivals, and a steady stream of hikers with heavy packs.

It was a place of haves and have-nots in every way you could imagine. Dogs chained too tight; dogs running free; children too skinny; children too fat; swimming-pool houses up on the hills that sank suddenly into the ground and shacks that had hung nearly perpendicular off hills, without fail, for two hundred years. Everything seemed too much or too little, until you looked closely and realized in the shadows of those extremes, just like in every other place, there were a hundred people living lives in between, making do with just more than enough. One of those people was Edie's grandmother.

Mrs. Coxe: eighty-four years young. Still prone to sulks and temper tantrums, as if she'd never learned her mood was something she could control.

She also had a tumor. A knockout punch in slow motion. Three months probably.

EDIE ROSE THE NEXT MORNING to find Mrs. Coxe drinking coffee at the living room window, looking out on the yard, where wisps of fog drifted over the overgrown grass. A morning ritual of sixty-some years? No. There was a black bear outside the window because Edie had put a heap of dog food on the porch in an attempt to lure Trixie home.

"What a treat," Mrs. Coxe said as she took Edie by the hand.

A bear! the size of a bear! It rambled off the porch, rubbed up against Edie's car, snuffed around for more food, then glanced back at the house. Edie retreated to the room's far wall.

Mrs. Coxe laughed. "It can't see this far," she said, then

pressed her nose up against the window glass. "I don't think, anyway."

Edie crept back toward her grandmother. The bear had moved to the far side of Edie's car and was doing who knows what. Probably leaving a bread-crumb trail for other bears to follow.

"My grandfather once traded ten pounds of flour for a black bear cub," Mrs. Coxe said, putting her arm around Edie and drawing her back to the window. How thin her grandmother's arm, how evident the bone! "Then he traded the bear cub for a rifle. Then he traded the rifle plus a broken plow for a wheelbarrow, a sack of sugar, and a kiss."

How folksy! How charming! How chatty the woman who has had her coffee! Could any of this be true?

"I'm sure it'll go away on its own," Mrs. Coxe said. "Just like your dog will come back on its own."

"Her name is Trixie," Edie said indignantly. "She's not an it—" Edie had hit a roadblock: cry or stop talking. She stopped talking; but then she cried anyway.

Mrs. Coxe walked out of the room, and Edie stopped crying. Apparently she'd needed an audience. How embarrassing. When Mrs. Coxe came back a moment later, she held a pile of photographs, which she extended toward Edie.

"Those are your great-great-grandparents," Mrs. Coxe said. "Our family has been in these parts more than a hundred years. So you can't be such a baby. Not about a bear and not about a dog. Not even about a human being."

Edie looked at the photos. Each small black-and-white picture showed a crowd of kids bookended by a man and woman who probably weren't as old as they looked. The woman was white and the man, definitely, clearly, positively—black.

Edie looked at her great-great grandfather, looked at his kids—little bit dark, little bit curly-haired, little bit Italian-seeming, really—and then she looked at her great-great-grandfather again. "I didn't know he was black," Edie said, trying to sound nonchalant, utterly and absolutely unsurprised, nothing that could make her sound insensitive or racist. Because she wasn't!

"Melungeon," Mrs. Coxe said. And then she added, "Elvis was Melungeon," as if that explained anything.

Edie nodded. Life was surprising. It could give you a bear rubbing up on your car one moment and the next give you news that made such a bear seem small.

She was black?

Not that she minded. But?

Was this a so-what situation or monumental? She was already in favor of equality for all, poverty for none, peace on the planet, act globally and locally, seven generations fore-thought, and all that jazz. She had, after all, just come out of a very solid liberal arts education and held both the idealism and the energy of youth.

But your history? Your people? That should be a point of pride. Ancestors in the struggle! Or was that appropriation at its heart? Oh God, Edie didn't know, she really didn't.

"Tom Hanks is a Melungeon," Mrs. Coxe said.

"But what's a Melungeon?" Edie cried.

Melungeons. Once thought to be the lowest of the low, but by 2015, like the newly trendy handmade items pouring out of the mountains and onto the Internet, they had become desirable, romantic even, with annual meetings and books of genealogy and more members than detractors. Melungeons were mountain people historically, shunned for looking different—darker than whites, lighter than blacks—unwanted by either. Some folks believed, insistently, that Melungeons were descendants of Turkish or Portuguese sailors abandoned along the Atlantic seaboard in the sixteenth century. That was what the Melungeon Unions—meetings of anyone who cared to be included—sometimes reinforced and sought to prove with their DNA tests and genealogical studies and visiting Turkish dignitaries. But most people believed the simplest truth: the Melungeons were the product of black and white and Indian intermixing.

"What I want," Mrs. Coxe said, tugging the stack of photographs back out of Edie's grip, "is a green burial and a home funeral. I don't want mold to grow on my body. Let it rot like it's supposed to. Tell your father."

That was how Edie met Michael. Mrs. Coxe called the Mountain Home Funeral Home, and he came right over.

MOUNTAIN HOME FUNERAL HOME, one of the longest-running black-owned businesses in the county, started by Michael Hendrix, Sr., in 1934. Now run by his great-grandson Michael Hendrix IV: only twenty-seven and the proprietor of his own mortuary business, specializing in environmentally sustainable practices and death midwifery—but also the regular stuff, if you want it.

He came to the house to explain what would happen. Mrs.

Coxe sat strangely silent throughout (Who is this woman? Edie thought. How can a person change so much from second to second?), and perhaps as a result, Michael kept glancing at Edie, talking more and more to her, while Edie studied him, until Mrs. Coxe finally snapped her fingers in front of Michael's face and said, "Talk to me, you bastard."

"It's the tumor," Edie said immediately, though God only knew if that was true.

But Michael just laughed, smiled at Mrs. Coxe, and directed his attention toward her until he said, "So that's it," then turned to Edie as if she were the punctuation at the end of his sentence.

"IS THERE SOMETHING TO SIGN?" Edie asked.

"There is," Michael said.

After Mrs. Coxe had signed her paperwork and paid up front, Michael asked to say a word to Edie, and so she walked him to his car.

"She understands," he said, "that I'll be the one to prepare her?"

"Prepare her how?"

"Her body," he said.

"I'm sure she understands. That's why we called you. What are you saying?"

"It's just sometimes . . . people think they aren't prejudiced, and they think they can handle"—he paused again—"a black man washing their body, but then suddenly they can't."

"Well, she'll be dead anyway, right?" Edie said, her voice rising in pitch. God, how she hated that.

"Right," he said and looked at her.

"So you mean me? Do I understand?"

"You and your family."

"We're not racist," Edie said. "My grandmother's black. Melungeon. Whatever." How convenient to have this information to wield! She was not a racist! How could she be! She kept going: "My father's grandfather was black. No, my grandmother's grandfather was black. My great-great-grandfather, or something, was black. Melungeon."

Michael laughed.

"What?"

"So you're black?"

"What do you mean, preparing the body?" Edie asked suddenly. She nearly stumbled right into him, as if her words were spewing her rather than the other way round.

Michael had a measured way, calm; he'd brought it home from Afghanistan, as good as any medal.

Edie felt the urge to touch his arm.

"I'll wash the deceased," he said, "and keep the deceased cool with dry ice and take care of the deceased, so that your family can spend time with the deceased. In her home."

Still Edie didn't absorb it; didn't picture what the future held. All she could think was how he kept saying "deceased." Was it polite or was it weird?

"That's what she wants, isn't it?" Michael asked. "To be at home?"

They were interrupted by a racket from the trees: nature's squabbles. They both swiveled their heads. When they turned back to each other, Edie nodded her head yes.

"You know Melungeon isn't the same as black," Michael said.

Edie hung her head sheepishly, lifted her eyes up to him—my God, was she flirting? "I don't really know anything about it," she said with a smile. She was flirting! How swift the shifting tides of her emotions! "I only learned the whole deal this morning."

"You learned this morning that your family is black?"

"I saw a bear for the first time, too."

"And you met me," Michael said, as he turned toward his car. Then he looked back over his shoulder and smiled.

Was he flirting?

"If you see a lost dog," she called out, too loud, "she's mine."

"Okay," Michael called back.

Why were they shouting? They weren't so far apart.

"I'll keep an eye out," Michael said more quietly. "I have your number," he added.

He was flirting, Edie thought. Wasn't he?

SOON MICHAEL WOULD BE on his computer reading Edie's blog; and Edie would be on her computer reading his.

**MY NEW APPA-LATCH-IAN HOME, BLOG POST, JUNE 19, 2015**

Wood rot is a good home for some. As is the human carapace better known as your skin. But what is a good home for a human?

Some would argue a good home is big, but they would be wrong. Most people, it turns out, don't know what's best for them. Not even close.

That is my opinion.

Anyway, my new home is . . . here!

For those of you who didn't know, I graduated last month, and now I have gone south to take care of my grandmother and work on a project for Half-Earth. (More on that later.)

The bad news is my dog, Trixie (I got a dog!) ran away. I am trying to believe she'll be home soon.

### Coffinman, blog post, June 10, 2015

*When you work with the dead, you sometimes forget they were once alive, though just for a moment, and then you call yourself back, and you say a little prayer to the universe and the family:*

*sorry*

*sorry*

*sorry*

*sorry.*

*When you work with the dead, you learn to be less afraid, because almost always, with rare exception, the faces of the dead are at worst neutral and at best happy. You learn that the brain, if it gets the chance, floods the body with euphoria at the moment of death. And that is the most comforting thing you ever learn about anything ever. Except it was rarely true in Afghanistan.*

*In Afghanistan they taught us to make sure the bodies didn't look too alive—it was worse for the families if the bodies looked too alive.*

#### MY NEW APPA-LATCH-IAN HOME, JUNE 21, 2015

My grandmother and I don't exactly know what to do with each other. Most of the time, when I'm not outside, I code and 3D model and dream of streams of animals crisscrossing the country in corridors of protected habitat all linked together. That is what Half-Earth is! Corridors of connected habitat. And I am making a virtual version to promote the real thing. Or, rather, I am making the Appalachian

Valley corridor virtual; and some other good citizens are doing the other bits. And we are going to make an awesome website and an app and maybe even a game to sell. And for this I get paid a paltry sum of money but it feels good. I am not a sell-out! (yet)

I still can't find Trixie. I put flyers everywhere—the woods, the mountains, the country club, the gas station, even a few abandoned outhouses. If only she could read!

I keep joking about Trixie, but I feel awful.

### Coffinman, June 23, 2015

*I always hated that saying—the eyes are the window to the soul. But you know freaking what, the eyes are THE way to know that someone has passed. They aren't just the window to the soul, they are the soul lens, the soul camera, the soul mirror. Which is not to say blind people look dead—they just have a different-looking lens.*

*Nobody died today. I am a little worried about the money.*

*Does this blog seem cold to you? Because I am going for irreverent but respectful—that's a thing, right? I am definitely not going for cold or cruel or uncaring. Tell me the truth, please.*

*That is, if anybody is even reading. Anybody?*

AND SO EDIE LEFT A COMMENT, Anonymous, that said simply: I'm reading. Thank you for sharing. Later she noticed a bunch of people who were obviously his friends also commented and she felt silly for believing he was alone.

ON SATURDAYS, Edie called her mother and her sister; on Sundays, she called her father. She worked seven days a week, went to bed early, and got up even earlier. Sometimes she heard from people who had come across her flyers and claimed to have seen a stray dog back behind the old Food Lion, or a stray dog up on the old buffalo trail, or a stray dog drinking out of a trough of dirty water by the entrance to the old mine. But nothing ever came of it.

Most days Edie went into the hills. She climbed trees, swam in the creeks, she saw one snake chase another, she watched a single ant pioneer up a blade of grass, she imagined the world underneath her and the world underwater, she put her face or her camera anywhere they would fit, and she kept an eye out and an ear open for Trixie—and for bears. She flew her drone where she couldn't go, and back home she watched the footage on her computer. Each day Edie learned more of the hills, and each night she built more of Virtual Valley.

Edie had spent half her childhood inside video games; she knew they could be as magical as the real world. (Once her mother, coming across her immersed in some computer simulation, had said, "Go outside," and Edie had replied, "I am outside" without even a thought.) Every piece of wonder Edie found in the mountains, she put into Virtual Valley.

She showed Mrs. Coxe her progress, and Mrs. Coxe praised her like a good grandmother.

Do you love me? Edie sometimes thought. But who asks a question like that? And why?

"WHAT CAN DO I FOR YOU?" Edie asked her grandmother each morning.

"Not a thing," her grandmother said.

Those were the early days.

———

FOUR YEARS AGO Edie had been on a drunken visit to New
Orleans, an experiment in bad behavior that fortunately had
no lasting consequences

three years ago she had been in bed naked for the first time,
with the boy who would become her boyfriend, sex preceding
love, but giving way to it, sex as a step toward love, toward
closeness, why couldn't it be

two years ago, she had been the only woman in the advanced
coding class, other than her professor, and for the first time she
had a mentor, a real role model

one year ago, she thought she had it, the future wrapped:
she would marry, have babies, make millions, stir revolution,
code for good, code for money, code for fun, love her boyfriend forever and ever, be loved by her boyfriend forever
and ever

Now she just thought: What happened?

And occasionally: What will?


EDIE AND MICHAEL met again when Michael came upon
her lying on the mountain ground: eyes closed, arms out,
crucifixion-style, though that wasn't how she meant it.

"What are you doing?" he asked.

Her eyes flew open and the truth came out: "Opening my
heart," she said.

"Is it working?" he asked, dropping down beside her.

"Hard to say."

And then he lay down and spread his arms, so close to her
he first brushed her shoulder and had to scoot more to the side,
to spread his arms wider.

Edie popped right up to her feet, but Michael didn't seem to notice; his eyes were closed.

"I like it," he said after a while.

"I'm supposed to be taking videos," Edie said, and when Michael opened his eyes and saw her standing, he stood, too. He picked up her drone, which had been lying next to her on the ground.

"With this?"

Edie nodded.

"Can I try it?"

Edie nodded again.

For God's sake, what was wrong with her? Couldn't she speak?

He flew the drone awhile, both of them watching it go, not talking, until eventually it crashed and he ran to retrieve it. (Later Edie used the video of the crash for an eagle's-eye view of dying midflight.)

"Is this for Half-Earth?" Michael asked when he returned with the drone, which was really nothing more than a fancy remote-controlled helicopter. Half-Earth, he said, as if it was perfectly normal for him to know! "I read your blog," he said when she looked surprised. So open! No shame! No sneaking! What she should have said was "I read yours, too," but what she actually said was "Wow, thank you. I mean, not thank you, I guess thank you for being interested." She paused. "If you were interested. Anyway. Thank you for reading it."

"Could I buy you a coffee? Sometime?" Michael asked.

"Sure, I'd like that," Edie replied.

Only later did she wonder what he was doing there. Was he looking for her?

### Coffinman, July 12, 2015

*It's nice to be home. I would fight for this landscape, these hills; I think most troops would. Maybe the military ought to be in charge of Environmental Protection. Just a thought.*

*People want to look at Appalachia like it's outsider art. Kinda crazy and kinda cool, a world created by an angry child. Maybe if the Appalachian Mountains had been painted the way the Adirondacks were we'd be seen differently. Luminous instead of ominous.*

*You could say this place is dying; but maybe it's just changing, maybe that doesn't have to be such a bad thing. Even at its worst, this has always been a second-chance landscape, adaptable. Reforested and rebuilt and rebirthed. Not all bad anyway.*

"WHAT CAN I DO FOR YOU?" Edie asked her grandmother.

"Not a thing," her grandmother said.

### MY NEW APPA-LATCH-IAN HOME, JULY 14, 2015

Did you know Virginia has fifty-five types of salamanders?

Lately I've been reading about trees and looking at trees and identifying trees—growing trees in Virtual Valley. Let me tell you. There are a lot of trees. Every bit of the world has been named and labeled it seems. Except it hasn't . . .

I always thought my grandmother lived in the middle of nowhere. Turns out she lives in the middle of everything. People of the north: beware your smug superiority!

Can be lonely though.

———————

FOR YEARS, EDIE'S LIFE had been a steady progression away from family—a natural part of growing up, she assumed. But since moving, she almost never talked to her friends; she talked only to her family. She had let go of her recent past—most of it, anyway—with shocking ease. It was her former vision of her future that she found harder to release. Like one long and ugly afternoon when she coded her unexpected ex into Virtual Valley, creating his and hers avatars, rubbing them up against each other like Ken and Barbie, then birthing three beautiful babies in a house that dwarfed the animal corridor. Trixie Belden lived there, too. All wrongs righted. Everybody with a private bath. Fantasyland. Edie had to force herself to get out of bed and delete it that night.

WEEKENDS, EDIE TOOK her grandmother on a round of (sad?) good-byes to various friends and neighbors. Edie didn't stay herself; it didn't seem right. Instead she dropped her grandmother off and picked her up, as if Mrs. Coxe were a preteen, dating but too young to drive.

"I've never been so popular," Mrs. Coxe said, cheerful enough.

SOMETIMES MICHAEL TEXTED:

> Do you think animals feel joy, the way we do, on a beautiful day?
> A lot of them do; I'm certain of it.

Or Edie texted him:

> Do you think an apology means anything if the person apologizing wouldn't do the thing they apologized for differently a second time around?

Yes.

I don't think it does.

It does. It just doesn't mean what you want it to mean.

Sometimes Michael teased:

You know you wouldn't have been friends with me back when
  you were just a white girl.

She refused to joke about it; she always answered indignantly.

But were they friends?

He never mentioned having that coffee. And neither did she.

VIRTUAL VALLEY GREW BIGGER and Mrs. Coxe grew stranger. She was losing vision in one eye, which made it hard for her to tell the space between things. She'd walk with her arm out and smack right into Edie if Edie wasn't watching. Her moods were variable, as was her lucidity. As was Edie's patience. Sometimes Edie spent long hours away from the house even though she knew she shouldn't.

Then one morning, Edie glanced out the window and saw her grandmother at the end of the driveway, looking out. Ahead of her was a green expanse of weedy fields and then the woods. Mrs. Coxe wasn't moving, but still Edie slammed the front door open, ran down the driveway barefoot, and grabbed her grandmother by the arm as if she'd snatched her from the road. They were both in their pajamas.

"What are you doing?" Edie asked, trying to calm herself.

"Just looking," Mrs. Coxe said. Then she turned toward Edie, teetering a little. "Can you give me something to look forward to?" she asked, and Edie nearly cried out in surprise.

"Of course," Edie said. "Of course I will."

"Right away," she added, though she had no idea how.

WHO WAS THE GRANDMOTHER Edie remembered? An irregular visitor Edie loved largely by default, which didn't make that love any less large. A regular gift giver, but of items obviously recommended by Edie's father, who was himself getting recommendations from Edie's mother, so that Mrs. Coxe became a purveyor of lip gloss, pocketbooks, and clothing that was just a little too young. It was inevitable, post-divorce, when Edie saw her father less, that she saw her grandparents less as well.

Before June, Edie had never even been to Virginia.

Her time with Mrs. Coxe was obviously a gift—anybody would say so. But nothing short of saving her grandmother's life could really feel like enough.

Every week Edie's father asked, how is she, and Edie said, the same.

"CAN YOU PUT ME IN YOUR GAME?" Mrs. Coxe said one morning as Edie worked at her computer.

"It's not exactly a game," Edie said. "It's more like a simulation."

"Can you put me in it?"

"A version of you? Living out in the woods?"

"Yeah, maybe you could build me a little house."

"Okay," Edie said; then she smiled. "I think you'll like it there."

"I'm sure I will," her grandmother said. "Something to look forward to," she said, and Edie jumped at the reminder.

It was soon after that Edie ordered the DNA kit. She had the idea to give her grandmother, with her limited future, the gift of understanding her past. When the kit came, Mrs. Coxe allowed herself to be swabbed with very little complaint.

THEN ONE DAY, there was Michael, at the house when Edie came home, sitting on the couch while Mrs. Coxe stood in front of him.

"Your grandmother wants to be buried at People's Burial Ground," he said as Edie walked in the door. Edie's face, which had lifted into a broad smile, stiffened. Edie didn't know what People's Burial Ground was, but clearly Michael didn't approve.

"Don't you want to be buried with Grandpa?" Edie asked her grandmother. "Where is he?"

Mrs. Coxe pointed dramatically across the room, and Edie, much to her embarrassment, gave a small scream, before she turned to follow Mrs. Coxe's finger, which was directed at a wooden box on the mantel.

It didn't help—or maybe it did—that Michael started to laugh and couldn't stop.

"I won't be there long," Mrs. Coxe insisted. "It only takes fifty years for a body to rot. Grandpa can come with me."

"Okay," Edie said, turning to Michael. "Can't we get her a plot?"

That seemed to sober him up. "Historically, People's Burial Ground has been for blacks," he said.

"Discrimination," Mrs. Coxe said.

"Oh my God," Edie said, glancing perilously at Michael, but his expression was somewhere between serious and amused.

"Isn't there somewhere else you could be buried, Grandma? Why do you want to be buried there?"

"I can walk there," Mrs. Coxe said. And maybe because they'd spent so much time together, just the two of them, Edie felt she understood. Who wouldn't want to be buried close to home. In these woods. On this land.

Edie turned to Michael, "We are . . ." she started, but stopped when Michael tilted his head and stared at her. She started again: "When you say historically it's been for blacks, does that mean nobody else can be buried there?"

"I can refund your money if you want," Michael said. "I'm sure someone else can help you do whatever you want."

"But my family's been here a hundred years," Edie said. "And we're Melungeon." She said the word tentatively.

Was she fighting him? Why was she fighting him?

"You've mentioned that," Michael said. He was not one to make speeches.

"I just want to make my grandmother happy," Edie said softly.

The impulse to please the dying was a strong one.

Michael shook his head. "It's not just a place to be buried. People who spent most of their lives . . ." He paused, then started again: "People who had to fight . . . that's their land. The only thing they ever owned was that plot of land. I won't do it." Then he stood and turned toward the door. "I can refund your money if you want," he said.

"No," Edie said, calling him back. "That's not what we want."

The impulse to please him was strong, too.

––––––––

COULD YOU TAKE ME THERE? Edie texted Michael that night.

??

People's Burial Ground.

I guess so.

But he didn't offer a time or a day and Edie didn't ask.

THREE DAYS LATER she was out in the valley when the text came in: Tomorrow, 10:30?

Perfect, she texted back.

IT WAS A SMALL PLOT—maybe a dozen gravestones, most leaning over and hard to read. Indeed not a long walk from her grandmother's house; yet Edie had never found it in her exploring. There were weeping willows all about, and Edie couldn't help but picture the bodies underground with the trees' roots reaching toward them, for them. As much as Edie sought comfort from the image—bodies merged into nature—she couldn't find it. This felt like a battleground, and death like something far more wet, and alive, than dust to dust had ever called to mind.

Edie pulled out her camera.

"Is that why you wanted to come here?" Michael asked as she took photos of each gravestone. "To put this in your game?"

"It's not a game," Edie said. "It's a simulation."

"Are you putting these people in your simulation?" Michael asked.

Edie put her camera down and looked at him. "Do you think I shouldn't?"

"I think you shouldn't," Michael said.

"Okay," Edie replied. She wanted to ask what she'd done wrong, but she was too embarrassed to admit she didn't know.

THEY DIDN'T TALK for a long time after that. Edie checked his blog day after day, but he never posted a thing.

"ARE YOU SCARED?" Edie asked her grandmother.

Mrs. Coxe shook her head, paused, then said, "Sometimes. It's like coming to the last pages of a great book. I want to read faster, but I don't want it to end."

Edie was scared. But who wanted to admit that?

"I'm glad I don't know what's going to happen," Mrs. Coxe said. "I'm glad there's still one mystery left—right up until the end."

"Something to look forward to," Edie said, though immediately she regretted it.

But Mrs. Coxe nodded. "Finally I'll know something," she said, and Edie smiled.

"You want me to haunt you?" Mrs. Coxe asked, and Edie said, "Sure, if you want to."

IT WAS THEN THE DNA results came, and Edie sat her grandmother on the couch to explain again what she'd done. "This is your DNA," she said as she handed the envelope to Mrs. Coxe for her to open, though when Mrs. Coxe struggled, Edie took it back again. That's how things were then: Edie wanting her grandmother to be capable but then lacking the patience to let her grandmother complete any task. It wasn't all good what Edie was learning about herself.

"What do you think we are?" Edie asked as she pulled out the piece of paper.

Mrs. Coxe shrugged.

"This is your DNA," Edie said again and then again. But Mrs. Coxe just shrugged.

"Look at that," Edie said, pointing toward a slice of the DNA pie chart.

"Hmm," Mrs. Coxe said.

Edie didn't know it yet, but whatever she was trying to do for Mrs. Coxe was too late. The grandmother she knew was already gone.

Edie looked at the papers herself. Europe, Asia, Africa.

She knew she was romanticizing. Still, she liked it.

She reached for Mrs. Coxe's hand, and Mrs. Coxe let her take it.

### Coffinman, August 25, 2015

*People often die at dawn, you know. Or at the changing of the tide. Morticians and midwives—woken in the night.*

*Sometimes I get to bury someone who lived a long life in which they loved and were loved. The friends and family left behind grieve, and I do not underestimate their sadness and their loss, but I envy them the purity of their grief. No anger over the circumstances, no sense of injustice, no feeling that life is unfair. I hate when people say, "No regrets"—as if we should forget all our screwups. I have a million regrets, and I'm not even thirty. I've done people wrong (if it was you—sorry), of course I have. You have, too! And you should regret it! But regrets don't have to ruin you.*

*Regretting is not the same as grieving. Grief is accepting what you can't change. Regret is accepting what you can.*

*But why does change have to be so hard?*

### Coffinman, August 26, 2015

*That was a tease. Stupid. What I'd change, what I want to change, will change, is how I take myself out of the world. I spend too much time alone. I choose to spend too much time alone. I sometimes think I am most myself alone—but it's easy to be good and noble and true when nobody is bothering you. Who you really are is who you are when other people are bothering you.*

*(joke) (kind of)*

*The one thing I know, working the job that I do, is while it might be okay to breathe your last breath alone—maybe preferable—you don't want to do your dying alone, and the people who do your dying with you, who don't desert you, who, in fact, embrace you—those people are your people. Doesn't matter what they look like or how much money they have or who they voted for, doesn't matter what their favorite movie is or what they did to you when you were young . . . those are your people.*

### MY NEW APPA-LATCH-IAN HOME, AUGUST 30, 2015

I've been reading about the Melungeons—which I'm one of. Which means some of my ancestors were black—confirmed by DNA! Not to be flip—I am well aware that my ability to adopt a symbolic ethnicity without any consequence is an aspect of my white privilege. (that sounded pretty smart, right?) (it's true though.)

Anyway, the Melungeons had it rough, I gotta say. They were

moonshining, horse-thieving, six-fingered, flying, dirty-kneed witches according to everyone who wasn't one of them. And worst of all, down here at least—they were inhospitable. But wouldn't you be if people were taking away your right to vote, stealing your land and kidnapping and sterilizing your women? Not surprising that Melungeons claimed to be Portuguese or Turkish when that made them white, which got all their rights back. Made sense back then. Not so much now. You're black, people, accept it.

What a world.

But Obama, right? I mean, progress, right?


"YOUR SISTER READ YOUR BLOG," Edie's mother told her.

"Great!"

"She's listening to rap music now."

"Is that a problem?"

Silence.

"Mom, is that a problem?"

"No, it's just weird."

"I mean, you're not a racist, right, Mom?"

"Of course not. You know that."

"And you wouldn't mind if my boyfriend was black, right, Mom?"

"Of course not. I'm a Democrat."

Edie laughed.

"Is your boyfriend black?" her mother asked.

"I don't have a boyfriend, Mom. I just wanted to make sure you weren't a racist."

"I'm from New York!" her mother said, and Edie laughed again.

———

THEN EDIE FOUND TRIXIE'S BODY. Maybe. What was left of it, of something. And she didn't know what to do, so she called Michael.

"I think maybe my dog is dead," she said.

"I'm so sorry," he said, no hint of annoyance or surprise in his voice, no residual of their last meeting lingering in his tone. "But you shouldn't give up hope. There's so much she could survive on out here. You still might find her."

"No. I think I did find her. I think . . ." Edie swallowed hard. "I think a coyote got her. Or a bear."

"Where are you?"

"In back of my grandma's house. I think maybe Trixie tried to come back and . . . I'm sure it's my fault, that bear . . . I think it's my fault."

"Stay there," Michael said. "Keep any animals away."

There was fur of the right color, bones of the right size, viscera of all kinds—the common dominator that could belong to anything, any body. But it made sense for Trixie to be there. Something had torn up the remains, eaten its share. It was an awful sight, and Michael spared Edie most of it. He gathered everything in his gloved hands, put it all in a biodegradable bag, and then dug a hole as deep as he could with a shovel Edie found in her grandmother's leaning-over shed.

It was the kindest thing anyone had ever done for Edie, but afterward, she couldn't stop crying, and finally Michael left her alone in her grandmother's arms.

"Child," Mrs. Coxe kept saying, "oh child. What are we going to do with you?"

THAT NIGHT EDIE texted Michael and asked if she could come over. And he said yes and she did, and she walked right into his arms and kissed him, and he put his hand up along her back, under her shirt, and God knows, a feeling went right up her.

EDIE DIDN'T TALK to Michael for a long time after that. He texted and he called, and finally she said she wanted a little space because she'd been hurt in the recent past, and her grandmother was dying, and her dog just died, and she didn't know what she was doing really, was that okay, and all he did was write back: yes.

SO WHY DID SHE do what she did?

**MY NEW APPA-LATCH-IAN HOME, SEPTEMBER 10, 2015**
I have discovered the best cure for a broken heart:
the world.
You lie on the ground and you let it all in.
Also, sex doesn't hurt.

SHE SHOULD HAVE DELETED that last bit. Really she should have.

The unexpected ex called her then. Of course he did. He wasn't immune—he wanted to be missed and mourned and never gotten over. At least for a little longer.

On the phone, Edie cried
and cried
and cried.
How embarrassing.

Also, her mother yelled at her. "Your Sister. Is Reading. Your Blog," she said.

"Cordelia knows about sex, Mom," Edie said. But still, she understood.

And, Michael. He mattered to her, and she was suggesting he didn't, and she knew he was reading, and she knew she would hurt him. So, why did she?

In truth, she didn't understand her own feelings. Was it Michael she liked or some idea of him? Or, worse, some idea of herself?

### Coffinman, September 20, 2015

*I get a hard time for being single. You know, a dude with his own business, a not totally terrible-looking dude. A credit to my family and all the rest. At least so the grandmas tell me. But life is easier alone. Isn't it?*

*I have seen more than my share of grieving spouses.*

"IT WAS JUST A JOKE," Edie texted him, but he didn't text back, not even to say, "What was?"

EDIE MEANT TO CALL HIM, she knew she had to call him, wanted to even. But she didn't. And she didn't. And she didn't.

Then, strangest of all, somehow completely unexpectedly, Mrs. Coxe died.

When the moment came—how to explain it from the outside? The only perspective that matters is the one we can never have.

Mrs. Coxe was dead. And what do the dead care about death?

IT WAS EARLY, not even eight a.m., but Edie called her father, then her mother, then Michael. She had no idea what she said to him really, but seemingly within minutes he was there, in the living room, with dry ice.

I hope I get a life, I hope I get a full life, Edie thought to herself. As if she hadn't had one already. Ingrate, she thought to herself.

"Do you want to keep her in the bed for now?" Michael asked. "Or bring her out front?"

"I think it's cooler in the bedroom," Edie said. "Is it hot out here? It feels hot." In her imagination, she had anticipated that she would be sad but calm, capable, able to execute the plan they had all spoken of without worry. But she felt panicked. Panicked and embarrassed by her panic. Death was a horror, a nightmare, she could not face it, she hated to face it. She had left Mrs. Coxe alone so fast she had to force herself back into the room, to make certain she was really dead.

"Perhaps we should take a moment. Let's sit for a moment, maybe in silence?" Michael suggested.

Edie nodded, and she and Michael sat on the couch, each taking the other's hand without even a thought, and Edie took a breath, so deep she knew he could hear it, but that seemed okay, Michael had become something to her, and maybe he had forgiven or never blamed her, or maybe he was just being nice because her grandmother died, but he was there, and she held his hand tight. Black white black white, their hands together. Of course she noticed. Noticing was okay. Wasn't it? She held his hand tighter.

In truth, Michael could forgive the living almost anything; it was something he'd learned from the dead.

They decided to leave Mrs. Coxe in her bed, until Edie's father could arrive that night and make what decisions he cared to. They packed her body in dry ice, and they arranged her clothes, and Michael tied her chin. And then, without even a pause, he kissed Mrs. Coxe on the cheek, and just like that, Edie's heart opened wide.

If her ex hadn't broken up with her, she would have gone west; Edie wouldn't have chosen her grandmother over him, she wouldn't even have considered it.

Good things born of bad. Edie could make a whole list if she had to. We all could, couldn't we?

She looked at her grandmother then. Her grandmother's body. Tied and tidied, an empty look on her face, not so much peaceful as absent. It was easy to see—her grandmother was gone.

A calm came down. Death was gone. Only the body remained.

"Now she knows something," Edie said, and Michael smiled. Maybe she did. Maybe she didn't.

Edie and Michael would marry one day. They have to, don't you think? Not for a long time, but eventually. It wouldn't always be easy—for the little reasons and the big ones, so much would happen in the years to come, the world to come.

Still, they made it. One day there were children then grand-children then great-grandchildren, until another day, death.

Edie would tell you it is life that needs looking after, not lives. The big picture.

Michael would say the opposite. Life, he thinks, ignores too much. Lives, after all, are not the same.

But either way—there through it all, forever and ever, in a virtual Appalachia, on a connected corridor, just outside the People's Burial Ground, is a small hut containing one never-ending grandmother and a bicolored border collie with a rough double coat—company for each other and company for us—at least as long as the power lasts.

# THE TROJAN WAR MUSEUM

The first Trojan War Museum was not much more than a field of remains. Dog-chewed, sun-bleached, and wind-blown bones, some buried, many burnt—but the Trojans prayed there, mourned their dead, told tales of their heroes, asked penance for their mistakes, pondered their ill fortune, poured their libations, killed their bulls, etceteraetceteraetcetera. There were not a lot of Trojans left; but, all the same, they hoped for a better future, and they believed in the gods, so they made sacrifices. Children, cattle, women, you name it.

Enter Athena. Motherless daughter, virgin version, murderer of Hector and Ajax and Arachne, at least a little bit.

*The dead added to the dead,* she said, *what do they expect us to do?*

Whatever the Trojans may have expected or hoped for, the gods did nothing.

The first Trojan War Museum was abandoned after a flood, a fire, an earthquake, not necessarily in that order.

The dark came swirling down. The city disappeared. Again.

SING TO ME NOW, *you Muses, of armies bursting forth like flowers in a blaze of bronze.*

SOLDIER: *I begged for sleep, and if not sleep, death. I was willing to settle for death. Then again, I've never felt more loved.*

*He looked at his father, a veteran; his grandfather, a veteran; his uncle, a veteran; his sister, a veteran; and he saw his future foretold, no different than birds and snakes foretelling nine more years of war.*

*Think: museums turn war to poetry. So to poets. So to war.*

*You know, Athena forgot Odysseus was out there.*

*O Muses.*

THE SECOND TROJAN WAR MUSEUM was built in approximately 951 B.C., upon the site of the first Trojan War Museum, after Apollo——boy-man beauty, sun-god, far-darter, Daphne-destroyer-and-lover-too——looked upon the empty plain dotted with the same old bones——more bleached, more burnt, more buried, more chewed——and declared it a ruin of a ruin and a dishonor.

*They are forgetting,* he told Zeus. *We must make them remember.*

Zeus——master of the house, lord of the lightning.

*You're not wrong,* Zeus said.

A museum run by gods is unusual, of course.

Ares argued for an authentic experience and so there was a room where one in ten visitors was killed and another in which vultures and maggots devoured the flesh of the rotting dead while dogs licked up their blood then turned upon each other.

The second Trojan War Museum did not last long.
The dark came swirling down. Again.

SOLDIER: *I HAD A MORE ORDINARY WAR. I feel lucky, really. Though sometimes, when I talk to other soldiers, I feel like it wasn't a real war and
so I'm not a real soldier.*

*Think: would you rather be told how to use what you've got or be
given what you want?*

*Think: would you want Achilles's choice or wouldn't you?*

*Think: glory?*

*History: a place for tourists to visit.*

*But what else could it be, really? The ever-present present?*

THE THIRD TROJAN WAR MUSEUM was built on Mount Olympus
in the approximate year of 602 B.C., when Zeus—suddenly
angry at the shifted tides of man's attention—gathered to
the cloud-white mountaintop those Trojan War mementos
that were readily at hand. (He was never one to go out of his
way.) Known first as Zeus's Museum or Zeus's Junk Drawer,
the collection only evolved into what came to be known as
the third Trojan War Museum under the guidance of the
more circumspect Athena—gray-eyed woman-warrior of
wisdom.

The museum labels provided insight into Athena's opinions.
Achilles's armor, for example, was identified as "Odysseus's
armor, won from Ajax after the death of its former owner, Achilles." The last item listed, and the culmination of Athena's display,
was noted only as: Horse comma Wooden. (Historians joke that

Zeus brought the horse to Olympus in twenty-two pieces and Athena put it together in twenty, just to show she could.)

Visitors were naturally limited to those with access to Mount Olympus, and so there were none. Enter again Apollo, literally, into the belly of the great wooden beast. Night and day, day and night, Apollo lay inside, golden knees curled to golden chest, as if he did not consider himself alone but, rather, crowded in with the men who had last huddled there, plotting brutality for the sake of civility. Apollo was interrupted only once when Poseidon—splitter of the sea, cracker of the coast, brother to the boss—popped his head up and in, swiveled it round, looked upon his nephew, and withdrew without comment.

Some historians believe Apollo's equine confinement to be the mere equivalent of a teenage boy shutting himself in his room (who is to say, given immortality, when a god hits puberty?), but he had with him a long scroll, the first written record of Homer's war, and he was studying it, particularly his own place in it—per Homer.

When finally he exited the belly of the ersatz beast, he went straight to his sister of sorts, the Curator comma Goddess, Athena.

*The poet has made fools of us,* Apollo said. *Except maybe you.*

*I'll look into it,* Athena said, taking the offending scroll from Apollo's hand.

Soon after, on his own pilgrimage to Delphi (where, after all, should a god in search of himself go?), Apollo posed his thought as a question: *Has Homer made fools of us?* The oracle replied: *The immortal is all.* And though he should have known better, Apollo heeded the words and not their meaning, taking comfort where it was not offered. At least, for a while.

But first, Poseidon, having exited the third Trojan War Museum unamused by Athena's celebration of her sometime-favorite Odysseus, opened the fourth Trojan War Museum upon an island he'd created for the purpose. For the first time, two Trojan War Museums operated simultaneously.

Poseidon arranged his island-museum with sculptures and fountains, each of gold. Achilles seaside beseeching his mother, Thetis; Iphigenia upon her pyre, testing fate; and largest of all, not-all-gifts-are-good Laocoön captured high above the water in the arms of Poseidon's serpent, mouth mid-scream, forever trying to prevent the future already past.

Offshore, Poseidon built a full-scale replica Greek ship, gold, with life-size gold sailors. And there Athena—arborist and arbiter, celibate celestial, and the museum's first visitor—got her revenge (part two) for Poseidon's past indiscretions in her temple by taking pleasure upon one of the more fully formed Myrmidons. (Though for the record, Athena remained, technically, virginal.)

The island had no plaques, no galleries of arms and armor, not even a building. Just Poseidon's golden dioramas and, running throughout, a pack of Horses (Live comma Wild).

It was surprisingly poetic.

There, too, was the iconic horse, this one gold. Though inexplicably it had its back to the surf; so that one had to ride backward to serve as sentry to the sea. And there, one morning, just so, was Apollo, the museum's second visitor.

*Remember when we built the walls of Troy?* he asked his uncle.

*Remember the rough stone and the cuts on our hands? Remember the pleasure of the task?*

Poseidon cupped a hand over his eyes to shadow the sun's glint off the back of the golden god.

*Was that the beginning?* Apollo continued as he gazed out upon the water, his hands upon the horse's golden rump.

In answer, Poseidon pointed a burly finger toward a dark-haired Beauty (Live comma Buxom) stripped and bound to a rock on the eastern edge of the island and said, *There's a girl if you want her.* Then he left without another word.

Apollo sat in the garden, backward upon the horse, for half a day.

He did not like how Homer had made him screech like a lust-for-blood cheerleader: Kill, you Trojans, kill. It hadn't happened. Not like that. Had it?

He did not like how he could not remember. It had seemed so important at the time.

He disliked, too, how the gods seemed such ill company. If they were not friends to each other, what friends did they have?

And when it came time for Apollo to depart? He transformed the maiden on the rock into one of Poseidon's horses. He thought it a kindness.

Still, she died with the rest of the herd, left untended without enough to eat.

The gods are not known for their sustained interest.

Soon enough the golden horse, the kneeling Achilles, the goddess-flavored Myrmidon, and all the rest ended up at the bottom of the bottomless depths.

The dark came swirling down. Again.

———

*THINK: WHAT ELSE are orders but dream-sent by gods?*

*Think:*

*1. Has the arrow left the bow?*

*2. If you were not fine, would you want to seem fine?*

*3. Desert or jungle?*

*In other circumstances, Patroclus and Hector would have been friends, don't you think?*

*SOLDIER: I don't like to talk about it.*

*SOLDIER: To fight for what you believe in—your rights, your independence, your country's rights and independence—means deprivations are gifts, the chance to prove your strength in the face of your oppressor. I welcome suffering.*

*SOLDIER: I said, I don't like to talk about it.*

*The time between then and now is nothing, the space between here and there—nothing, the only prophecy you need is the past.*

*Once Homer's war was found written on a mummy.*

THE FIFTH TROJAN WAR MUSEUM, the first to be widely known and visited, was opened in 1816 in Hampstead Heath.

Paris's helmet strap snapped by Aphrodite so that Menelaus could not strangle him, Menelaus's shattered sword, his leopard skin, the spear with which Hector killed Patroclus, a golden urn containing Patroclus's crushed bones, the girl's costume worn by Achilles when his mother hid him among Lycomedes's maidens.

All displayed under glass, available for viewing at a pound a head. People came in droves.

None of it was real.

Oliver Godlenstone, a retired British banker who'd spent

his youth crisscrossing the Middle East with a notebook and a small shovel, claimed to have personally dug these items from the earth of an undisclosed location, but in truth he had bought them from a man named Johan Turnkenman, who also claimed to have personally dug them from the earth of an undisclosed location. Godlenstone, despite his own lies, believed Johan Turnkenman's.

Explorers must trust in the hospitality of strangers; it is the only way to venture into the unknown world. And ancient strangers were often received with hospitality, the very hospitality invaders took advantage of.

The fifth Trojan War Museum had its wooden horse as well. There was an observation deck on its back, soon famous for after-hours assignations, many conducted by an increasingly earthbound and melancholic Apollo, a son never meant to surpass his father, a boy-god meant never to become a man.

Eventually the fifth Trojan War Museum came to Zeus's attention, and though he had done nothing with the actual artifacts still stored upon the cloud-white mountain, he did not care for fakes and forgers, and so he struck the fifth Trojan War Museum, in particular the observation deck of the fourth Trojan War Horse, with a bolt, effectively burning the entire estate down.

The dark came swirling down. Again.

But Apollo had an idea.

*Athens 1821*: He watched Greek soldiers throw enemy corpses into the well of Asclepius, Apollo's own son who raised the dead and in so doing died by Zeus's lightning. And he watched Turkish soldiers do worse.

*Crimea 1854*: Apollo glimpsed the lady with her lamp at the Scutari hospital as the dying reached out their hands and called her sister.

*Gallipoli 1915*: Apollo watched the Turkish and Anzac troops throw food and cigarettes to each other during lulls in their shooting.

There was more. Much the same.

SOLDIER: *I've never felt more significant than when I was in combat, but really I've never been more insignificant.*

SOLDIER: *I think if we could have gone home together—like the boys in earlier wars, who were all from the same town and stayed together and fought for their homes and went back to their homes—together—I think if we could have gone home together, we could have helped one another. But we got spread everywhere. The battalion was my home, and I fought for it, and when I left I didn't really have a home anymore.*

*Tell me: who will build the memorial to those who died in a pile of the dead, thrown there while still alive? Who will memorialize those shot with their hands in the air? Who will mark the grave of limbs?*

*A lot of people are really angry.*

*Think: shouldn't the immortals hold the world's memory? Why else immortality?*

*Remember:*

*The overwhelming stench. The bone which did not withstand the blow. The twelve-boy blood price for Patroclus's funeral pyre. The scale which weighed Hector's fate.*

———

IN 1986, APOLLO declared that he would open the sixth Trojan War Museum, known herein for reasons soon to be apparent as 6A.

*It will be the book of the soldier's coded heart,* Apollo told Athena.

*Go for it,* Athena replied.

*I want to learn what I am willing to die for,* Apollo added.

*Great,* his sister replied.

He meant to convey the soldier's experience to the non-soldier, the enemy's experience to the other enemy, the home-front experience to those on the war front; he meant to exhibit the wind, and the heat, and the cold, and the soldier's devotion, the soldier's fear, the soldier's courage, the soldier's boredom, the soldier's rage, the soldier's sadness, the soldier's interest, and the soldier's indifference. For once, a god meant to understand mankind. He wanted to display the human soul. But also soldiers' bones chewed by dogs.

Apollo enlisted the interest of Olympus in his planning, and 6A turned into a research institute. This became the gods' scientific age, in which they conducted experiments by appearing in people's dreams and determining how best to change the course of human behavior. They conducted a test in which they saved the lives of every person engaged in battle for seven years running. It was a war without casualties. It went on without end.

6A lasted sixteen years, though with not much to show for it.

And still Apollo felt false. What he wanted was to be a soldier, to hold the museum of experience inside his own heart.

The dark came swirling down.

———

*BAGHDAD, FALLUJAH, RAMADI, TIKRIT. Apollo went to war.*

*Think: which side did he choose?*

*But: are there only two sides?*

*When you are immortal, how to prove that you are brave? What else to risk but your life?*

*Whenever Apollo stepped in to save his men, fate refused his effort. They died anyway, or worse.*

*Think: worse?*

*Shall I go on?*

*Soldier One killed Soldier Two in Place A; Soldier One killed Soldier Three in Place B; Soldier One killed Soldier Four in Place C; Soldier Five killed Soldier One in Place C. Soldier Six killed Soldier Seven and Soldier Five in Place D. Soldier Six made it home to die a later death.*

*Pop quiz: what happens when you replace Soldier One with Soldier Six?*

*Hector thought there was glory in the sight of burial mounds. He thought that men of the future looking upon them would think: There lies a man killed by Hector. And so they did sometimes.*

*How much suffering brings the end to arrogance?*

*Sack the city, kill the men, take the women.*

*Think: glory!*

SOLDIER: *You learn to believe you can do things—drugs, sex, killing—that are separate from your life and separate from who you are, that those things will stay with the fight. But then you try to go back to your life and who you are—who you think you are—and you're not that person anymore, you're those things you did.*

SOLDIER: *I do not want your gratitude.*

*Think: would you want your boredom punctuated by terror? Or would you want your terror punctuated by boredom?*

*Apollo went to war and he went to war and he went to war and he went to war. Each time he came home, he went back.*

*Who is the god of the IED and the RPG? Who is the god of Agent Orange, and heroin, and twelve-year-old prostitutes? Who is the god of orders gone wrong, ill-thought, ill-executed, and ill-reported? Who is the Mad god? Far-darter without aim, healer without heal-ing. Time went untracked—dream, memory, prediction—all the same. A woman shot. A child shot. A soldier shot. A bow, a bomb, a gun, a knife, a gas, a drone. Dead wounded dead. An old man-woman a young manwoman an indeterminate manwoman was that a manwoman what was that a dog? The details different and all the same.*

*In the end, Achilles fought not for Agamemnon or Helen or Greece, nor even for Patroclus, but for Patroclus's death.*

HOW TO MEMORIALIZE the soldiers' bodies? Those carried down the hills of Gallipoli upon a flood, the soft bodies of the long dead left in the fields of Antietam, the exploded bodies of the Middle East?

The constant light of the corpse fires? Bodies stomped into mass graves, the symbolic soldiers chosen for the tombs of the unknown, Union soldiers in Mrs. Lee's rose garden, armies made of terra-cotta? Trees and flowers and blocks of stone? Apollo did not care for any of these options.

The only way to make people understand death was to kill them.

6B, known until now as the Lost Trojan War Museum, opened along the Dardanelles, in the year 2025.

The first object seen upon entering was the arrow Apollo guided into Achilles's heel. The next object was the decapitated head of the museum's last visitor. That display changed regularly.

Athena quickly stopped it. Apollo retreated from the Earth, leaving behind only a wooden horse full of corpses.

The dark came swirling down, darker, and again.

THE DESIRE TO GIVE IN TO FATE, *the desire to give in to pleasure, the desire to give in to madness, the desire to give in to anger, the desire to give in to despair, the desire to give in to desire.*

*Interstitial anger.*

*Darkness in the god of light.*

*Apollo kept eternal youth and added endless experience.*

*Museum,* mouseion, *seat of the Muses, a place of contemplation or philosophical discussion.*

SOLDIER: *I wanted to come home and lead and serve at home as at war. But nobody wants me to serve and lead; they want the wounded warrior they can put on parade.*

SOLDIER: *You go to war thinking you're putting your body at risk, but really it's your soul.*

*The soldiers in the rear didn't carry rifles, for it was assumed they would pick up those of the soldiers who fell in front.*

*The mothers and fathers of war do not have sons and daughters, they have soldiers, with whom they, too, could go to war, couldn't they?*

*Think: what else is war but human sacrifice?*

SOLDIER: *Sometimes you're okay. And then nobody believes you.*

*The Parthian shot. A boar's-tusk helmet. The oak of Dodona whispering prophecies. The lists of Linear B. The figure-of-eight shield and the silver-studded sword. The well-manicured battlefield. The desecration of a sacred space.*

*Words are the worst thing to tell the story of war, but how else to make myth?*

*Did you know* homeros *means hostage, Zeus's bucket of thunderbolts is never empty, and the cypress is the tree of mourning?*

SOLDIER: *Eventually you stop testing yourself and you start testing God.*

*Think: are the dead safe?*

*The whole story could come only from an interrogation of millions.*

SOLDIER: *How you die, that's how you are forever, that's how you go into eternity? And what you said, that's all the world is left with?*

*Everlasting last words.*

*Homer's words have outlasted us already.*

*If you can stand it, the unburied will come to you and prophesize.*

THE SEVENTH TROJAN WAR MUSEUM opened in Times Square in 2058; it was run by an American and silent-partnered by Aphrodite in high-heeled human form. The seventh Trojan War Museum had donors and blockbuster shows and a gift shop that turned over thousands of dollars a day. A marble statue of Paris loomed over the lobby. A nude of Helen dominated each brochure. Every fifteen minutes, dozens of ticket holders climbed up into the horse's belly and sat in the dark, crowded and sweating, until the next quarter hour's crowd was due to be let in.

The line for the oracle was so long a series of challenges were set along its twisting path.

The biggest seller in the gift shop was the tear-collection bottle. The second was the Trojan condoms.

But then, after just a few months, the riots came. The oracle stood accused. The museum, Times Square, swaths of New York City were destroyed.

And the dark came swirling down.

THE EIGHTH TROJAN WAR MUSEUM, the current Trojan War Museum, is such a mystery. It opened its doors unexpectedly in a small town along the Aegean coast on July 9, 2145. Even the gods aren't sure who started it. They have begun to wonder if there is some force larger than them. It's been around nine years now, which is pretty long for a Trojan War Museum.

Visitors often cry in the eighth Trojan War Museum.

To enter, you must travel a long path to the underground. Some people can't seem to leave. Or they come back repeatedly.

You can touch anything in the eighth Trojan War Museum; there are no glass barriers or alarms or even guards to stop you. Though what you touch might burn or bite or weigh on you. Sometimes what appears to be an ordinary sword turns out to be a piece of someone's soul that once picked up cannot be put down. Sometimes a wind will blow in the eighth Trojan War Museum that will pin an unsuspecting visitor in place—sometimes it will hold them there for more than an hour, regardless of their pleas. But an hour is nothing compared to the weeks ships sat in the Dardanelles waiting for the wind to change.

At the eighth Trojan War Museum, there is a room of lost languages, indecipherable symbols, and unidentified emotions.

It is rumored that the terminally ill can come to the eighth Trojan War Museum to choose death, that the Nereids will provide escort, and that there is a garden of bodies, a common but contented grave.

People sometimes disappear for more than a year and reappear in what is commonly known as the room of return but is really the lost and found.

The eighth Trojan War Museum seems to have a mind of its own.

Sometimes it wraps visitors in mist; one day perhaps it will not let us go.

There is a room for those who want to forget that allows them to forget; perhaps one day it will make us all forget.

Children left in day care are turned into a flock of birds and taken on a guided flight. Perhaps one day they will not be brought back.

The eighth Trojan War Museum has no wooden horse; and I wonder if that is our biggest clue. If the museum is the horse, then we are in the hours of peace between pulling the beast inside the city walls and the city being sacked.

I am not the only one who wonders. It is why the history of the Trojan War Museums has become so important.

Some say it is Apollo again, still trying. I fear the eighth Trojan War Museum might be run by Nemesis—true mother to the Circean Helen—spirit of fate and divine retribution, the ultimate ender of arrogance.

But even so.

If history is fate, we know what will happen, don't we?

It is rumored that the ninth Trojan War Museum has begun

already; Hades is preparing it in his underworld, a museum of the dead for the dead, a museum we can all visit one day, though not before our time.

But that will not be the end.

Because finally

after the over and over

there will be the tenth Trojan War Museum.

Have you heard of ephemeralization? The process of building more and more out of less and less? The tenth Trojan War Museum will not have a building, nor any objects, nor any visitors. It will be the air we breathe. Unavoidable. Born in us like instinct. A story we already know and need never tell again.

The After War instead of the Ever After War.

The true Trojan War Museum.

What are the odds?

Now there are buttercups upon the Trojan plain.

# GOOD FORTUNE

>>> ————————————————————————————————→

**I. If you put the changeling in the fire and the changeling goes up the chimney, the human child will be returned.**

When the first note was found, Gudrun Tabak took it too seriously. The police came, the hotel owners were notified, the hotel guests warned, and Gudrun slept with her vegetable knife in her fist every night, just in case.

The hotel, located some sixty miles north of Miami along the Atlantic coast, catered especially, though not solely, to birth tourists—foreigners who appreciated the U.S. Constitution enough to know that the Fourteenth Amendment granted any child born in the U.S. American citizenship. These were no crawled-under-the-fence-and-over-the-border immigrants sacrificing themselves for second-generation children; they were wealthy parents who wanted dual-citizen babies and could afford to spend months at a luxury hotel in South Florida, paying the full cost of hospitalization and so on. It was Gudrun's job to make sure these guests, who represented a small portion of the hotel's population but a significant percent of its profit, were satisfied.

Each day Gudrun dressed in an unofficial uniform, white shirt and black pants, lived with her phone clipped to her belt, and kept no boundary between her life and her work. Some days after too many complaints—too few babysitters, too much gluten, Florida was too hot and too wet—she would find a corner, close her eyes, and think, *White shirt black pants, white shirt black pants,* to calm herself. But most days she went from want to want without complaint: problem solved problem solved problem solved.

Some days it felt like a regular hotel. Other days Gudrun looked at the wing of long-term suites and felt the pulsing thoughts of a hundred and thirty-two past and present babies swaddled in their twist-turned fates.

She'd worked there nineteen years. Nineteen years and what to show? A hundred and thirty-two babies and their pampered parents. Nineteen years gone. Like a disappearance. One day she was forty-three.

THE FIRST NOTE was so vague as to be both threatening and ridiculous. "You will be found out." Like a horoscope, something that could apply to anyone. It had been slipped under the door of a recently emptied suite and discovered by the thought-to-be-Russian housekeeper, Larisa Rusak. It could have been meant for the incoming guest, or the just-left guest, or, as most of the long-term guests speculated, put under the wrong door and meant for one of them.

It was summer in South Florida, too hot to move beyond the shaded tiki bar if you even came out of your air-conditioned room, yet gossip ran in a tight circle around the hotel. Everybody had a theory they pushed involving someone else, and a second theory they kept secret involving themselves.

Suite 210 thought she could be found out for one of three things and ranked them one to three in order of preference. Suite 211 wondered if she could have a secret so secret it wasn't even known to her. The husband of Suite 119 had a suite for his wife and a suite for his wife's mother and another suite for his mother, who didn't like that his wife's mother was there, and one last suite for his mistress, who was also having his baby. He didn't stay more than a few days at a time himself. Any one of them could be threatening another.

Larisa Rusak, the thought-to-be-Russian housekeeper, who found the note, was actually an undercover journalist from Ukraine, investigating reports that Russians were giving birth to Russian-American citizen-babies in order to raise them in America as Russian spies. Understandably, Larisa Rusak thought the note was for her.

Gudrun, too, had her secrets: a young divorce, a few ridiculous years, a black feeling in her heart. Maybe the note was hers?

Because she was on call seven days a week, twenty-four hours a day, Gudrun lived at the hotel, in a small apartment over the front office, which was its own small building. The police searched Gudrun's apartment thoroughly after she (she!)

called in the first note. They were polite about it. They found nothing of interest. They asked about David, though; they searched his apartment, too.

Probably everyone suspected David—the piece that didn't fit.

He lived in the apartment next to Gudrun's, which belonged to the hotel owners, who lived most of the time in Turkey.

David: Gudrun's twenty-four-year-old nephew, who'd come into existence only four months earlier when he'd e-mailed Gudrun to ask if she was related to Balsan Tabak, who he believed to be his father.

She was.

Balsan was Gudrun's older brother, who had been paralyzed, more than paralyzed, erased really, twenty-four years earlier, in a car accident that also killed two women. Both women were well into their eighties; it would have been easy to think the accident was their fault (their car was turned to shrapnel), but Balsan drove too fast, always. It was a joke among everyone who knew him. A joke, of all things.

At the time, Gudrun had been a sophomore at Penn, where Balsan was a star MBA student. After the accident, she stayed in Philadelphia with Balsan's ghost while her parents moved back to Turkey with Balsan's paralyzed body and damaged mind. America became Gudrun's parent then, and it looked after her well enough—with its grocery stores, libraries, modest employment opportunities, and endless television programming.

In Turkey, Gudrun's mother cut her hair brutally short; her father grew fatter and fatter and let his beard run wild. Only

Balsan remained immaculate, so much devotion turned on him, as it always had been, really. Then one by one they died, first Gudrun's father, then Balsan, then her mother. It took years, but it seemed instantaneous.

At the time of the accident, neither Gudrun nor her parents knew about Balsan's pregnant girlfriend, who in her own grief and youth and fear never told Balsan's family about his (her!) (their) baby. When that baby, the suddenly twenty-four-year-old David, in custody of his heretofore hidden-in-plain-sight birth certificate, decided to seek his father's family out, he, easily enough, found Gudrun Tabak.

First there were months of e-mails, then an abrupt two-week silence, then David, along with a previously unheralded, very visibly pregnant, very visibly young woman, showed up at the hotel's front desk. Gudrun knew immediately who he was. Balsan reborn, same age and everything.

"It's a boy," this new Balsan said with a wry smile.

What was the son of your nephew, Gudrun wondered absently as she stared at the pregnant girl. Your great-nephew? Grand? Layers upon layers of family suddenly. Was that what she was looking at?

"She's my half sister," David said.

Gudrun had never been good at hiding what she was thinking.

"Her boyfriend's a bastard," David said.

Joanna, the half sister, looked at the floor.

"Okay," Gudrun said, and that was that.

They'd been there three weeks when the first note was found.

———

"YOU WILL BE LUCKY and I will be rich, and one will always take care of the other," Balsan had told Gudrun once.

"So I will be poor and you will be unlucky," she'd said in reply. How she had laughed at the time.

Gudrun had thought her personality, a mellow but open-hearted optimism, was a set thing until the day of Balsan's accident, when a kernel of bitterness, a baseline outrage, was inserted inside her and never left.

An ordinary accident with endless consequence.

DAVID LOOKED LIKE BALSAN, much as Gudrun remembered him; and he was curious about Balsan. He asked about Balsan, and Gudrun tried to tell him what she remembered. "He was special," she said, though she knew it was the kind of thing people always said of the dead. But he was.

Wasn't he?

Once in the night, as a baby, Gudrun looked out through the iron bars of her crib (wood! surely they were wood) and saw the five-year-old Balsan staring at her, an orange glow emanating all around him.

Gudrun did not mention that to David.

Balsan, the natural center to every group. Born to be elected. America's dream.

This did not mean he was good. He'd treated their parents like easy marks, used people as portals to worlds he wanted. There'd been rumors, too, in high school: girls he'd treated badly, worse than badly. One girl especially, who left school and never came back. But Gudrun had thought Balsan would change—grow out of his shallow longings and selfish behavior into a person who would do great things. She'd thought he had changed. But then, so suddenly, his story had ended, and her long sense of incompletion began.

The ordinary consequence of an endless accident.

She should have been the one to change, done great things herself, but she hadn't.

WHEN THE FIRST NOTE was found, it was David that the Russian/Ukrainian housekeeper/journalist brought it to.

"PLEASE DON'T SLEEP WITH THE STAFF," Gudrun told him. "They'll quit, or sue, or somebody will get pregnant or something."

"I'm not sleeping with Larisa Rusak—that's not why she did it," David said.

But then why did she?

THE JINN ON Gudrun's left shoulder said: Don't Trust Him.

The jinn of her right said: You Have To.

David hadn't given her any reason not to trust him.

It was the note that made her wonder.

"LARISA?" GUDRUN SAID, tracking the housekeeper down in a long-term suite one morning. "If you find anything else, bring it right to me, okay?"

"Of course," Larisa Rusak said without lifting her head from the tub she was scrubbing.

She was quite a well-read housekeeper; Gudrun had noticed that. Always slipping a hotel newspaper into her bag at the end of the day. But Gudrun was used to foreign women with good educations suffering underemployment.

DAVID AND LARISA RUSAK had slept together, but only the once. So what; they wanted to.

THE RUSSIANS WEREN'T REALLY making American-citizen-baby-spies. Though it wasn't out of the realm of future possibility.

IF YOU VIEW DEATH as a bad end, then we are all ill-fated. Could Balsan's accident be seen as anything other than a tragedy? Would you have to believe in the Eternal Heaven, the Garden of Eden, the Promised Land, Valhalla, the Elysian Plain, Vaikuntha, Tir Na Nog, Paradise, Nirvana, Shangri-la, Canaan, Zion, Kingdom Come, and the Pearly Gates to believe it was anything but a tragedy?

Gudrun had finished college, married young, divorced soon after.

When her father died, then Balsan, then her mother, she shut the door on her heart. Except sometimes she was locked inside, warm and alive but alone, and sometimes she was locked outside, cold and stone but surrounded by people.

It is a terrible thing to fear both death and life.

"DON'T YOU WANT A FAMILY?" Gudrun's young husband had said to her once.

"I already have a family," she said in return.

"You mean your dead parents?" he said.

He'd meant well, really. Believe me, he did.

She should never have married him, but she wished she'd been kinder.

Some lessons must be learned over and over; some stories told more than once.

ONE DAY LARISA RUSAK left work and never came back.

## II. Humans are made from clay, jinn from the fiery wind.

The second note read: If you do not pay fifty thousand dollars a year I will steal your baby and rape or kill or sell it as I wish.

It was found by the wife of a Turkish diplomat (Suite 119), and the police took her hysterics seriously. The wife paid her bill and flew back to Turkey with a baby only three days old.

A flaw in the blackmailer's plan, David joked, but Gudrun wondered if maybe that had been the plan, to scare the woman away.

The rival hotel in Miami had long done long-term stays for plastic surgery patients, but more recently rumors had sprung up of significant quantities of extravagantly beautiful, pregnant Eastern European women poolside, rumors Gudrun easily confirmed with a trip of her own, when she stood in the blazing sun and witnessed a lineup of bikinied pregnant perfection, all wavy hair and taut belly bumps, as dreamy as a mirage.

"Maybe it was them," David said, "stealing our business." He had begun saying things like "our," as if he and Gudrun (and Joanna) were partners in something.

"Could be," Gudrun said, though she didn't really believe it. She was rattled. Who threatened to rape a baby?

THE RIVAL HOTEL in Miami was stealing their business. Though through much more ordinary methods, like advertising and word of mouth. Birth tourism was booming. Anchor babies abounded.

The dream is to be an American, so that you can achieve the American Dream, which is to become someone better than who you were born.

So you are already dreaming the American Dream before you are an American.

Why shouldn't these parents use their one superpower—purchasing power!—to get their children the most they could?

Too many believe that one thing must come at the cost of another.

GUDRUN COULD HAVE held dual citizenship, gotten a Turkish identity card, had a Turkish identity—why hadn't she?

Because Turkey was the dream, ethereal and unknown. America was the opportunity, and she took it.

**III. Sometimes the changeling is not the child of a fairy, but an ancient fairy come to the human world to die.**

The third note read: Your firstborn belongs to me.

It was left under Gudrun's door.

Like a curse in a fairy tale, Gudrun thought. Then she

laughed; she was forty-three, after all. Too late, she thought. At least, probably.

She showed the note to David, who paled but said nothing.

"This is out of control," Gudrun said. "I'm calling the police again."

"No," David said. "What do you think they'll do other than search our rooms? Or, worse, try to shut down the hotel."

That was a concern, of course. If they could find just one woman who'd lied on her visa forms, the police could cause a lot of trouble.

"You didn't write it, did you?" Gudrun said.

What she meant was, Can I trust you?

"How can you even ask me that?" David said.

"Because I don't really know you!" Gudrun said. She stepped inside her heart and slammed the door. Warm and alive and alone.

"Maybe it was Joanna's boyfriend," David said. "He threatened to kill her if she didn't get an abortion."

"Maybe you both should go then," Gudrun said.


THE SECOND NOTE was written by the husband of the woman who received it, the Turkish diplomat. As you know, by strange coincidence—or his stupidity—his wife and his mistress were pregnant at the same time, and he paid for both of them to have their babies in the U.S. The mistress was supposed to go to the rival hotel in Miami (that way the husband could travel between them), but she hadn't because she'd found out which hotel the wife was at. The husband needed one of them to leave; he wrote the second note. The first note gave him the idea.

He got away with it. Nobody ever knew the truth, except you and me, and him.

What did the mistress think when she saw the wife's hysterics, heard of her departure?

"What good fortune."

Rich, lucky, how cruel we can be.

DAVID KNOCKED ON Gudrun's door late on the night of the third note. So late that she answered holding her vegetable knife in her hand.

Prayers should be said during the day, when if-there-is-a-God is awake. Stories should be told at night, the time of dreams.

"Please don't make us leave," David said.

Gudrun let him in.

DAVID (AND JOANNA) had a mother (of course), who it seemed they had abandoned, leaving town without saying for where, and ignoring her calls until she stopped making them. They had every plan to get in touch with her eventually, presumably after she'd suffered enough—more, at least. She wasn't a bad mother, really. She just hadn't handled the news of the pregnancy very well. Though that was for her own good reasons, due to her own past history.

"BUT WHY ARE YOU HERE?" Gudrun asked David finally.

"I couldn't wait any longer, to tell you the truth."

"No, not right-now here, here at all, at-the-hotel here."

David looked at her a little blankly.

"What do you want from me?" Gudrun cried out.

"I thought you could help with the baby," he said. "Because you know about babies."

She'd seen a hundred and thirty-two babies born, some from right there in the hospital delivery room. Each one she'd tapped on the nose while saying, "Hello, baby." A good-luck spell of her own invention.

"You and your hotel," David said, "it seemed like fate. I found you just when I needed you."

Balsan never needed her. Not that he admitted.

"We're family, right?" David said.

PERHAPS IN TURKEY was some museum of mementos that held Gudrun's past—the toys and photographs and clothing of generations of her family. But she owned nothing she could pass down to David; all she could give him was the stuff of actual memory.

First she told him the story of Balsan's accident, then two more.

One was a story Balsan told Gudrun not long before his accident. It went like this: Once there was a man whose first wife was a human and whose second wife was a jinn. With his jinn wife he had five invisible children, and with his human wife, he had nine visible children. The five invisible children were a great help to him in his industriousness. The nine visible children seemed inadequate by comparison. The nine visible children grew jealous, though they knew not of what. One day, in their jealousy, they burned down the house, with the invisible children inside.

"So, Gudrun," Balsan had told her, "you never know what's really happening."

He always made his own morals.

"And you don't know a goddamn thing about me," he added angrily.

They had been fighting. She had been trying to be the responsible one, age nineteen. She had told him he was self-centered, obsessed with money, and a fool.

How she missed him.

Maybe he was right. You never know what's really happening. So don't burn down the house. Even if you wish to see the sky.

SECOND WAS A STORY that Gudrun's father told her once, which had been told to him once, by his own father. Gudrun's father told it to her over the phone, from far away, after the accident, just before she never saw him again.

Gudrun's grandfather had been a boy in Ordu, along the Black Sea, when an Armenian boy who'd lost his parents came to live with his family. Many Armenian orphans were placed in Turkish homes during this time. (It would be years before the grandfather understood that the orphans' parents had been killed by the government.) The two boys lived like brothers. And then one day the Armenian boy was gone. (It would be years again before the grandfather understood that fear of reprisals had led the government to kill the children they had at first spared.) In the in-between time, when the boy was missing and his fate unknown, the grandfather invented many stories and adventures for his lost brother. He gave his brother a grand fantasy to live inside. But he himself lived in fear. How could he not? Here one day, gone the next?

GUDRUN GAVE DAVID these stories. The family inheritance. Not much, but the truth anyway.

And what did Gudrun inherit?

David, of course.

THE THIRD NOTE was left by a writer who'd been staying in the hotel for two weeks in order to finish his novel. He wanted to be part of the story.

JOANNA HAD THE BABY. David and Gudrun helped her. David and Joanna called their mother, and she helped them, too. Gudrun liked her, David's mother, Balsan's girlfriend, the one time they met.

Life went on. More babies. More years.

Is that all?

Yes and no, forever and ever.

Before: a nephew-stranger, a brother-replacement, an old beginning.

After: still fear but less, still stone but less, still Gudrun but more.

AND THE TRUTH ABOUT the first note? "You will be found out?" I am not sure I even want to tell you, it's so absurd, such a meaningless coincidence with which to begin or end a tale.

But the truth about the first note is this: a thirteen-year-old girl—the oldest daughter of an older woman on a second marriage and pregnant with twins—wrote it. She'd copied the idea out of a book she'd read. A prank, but an angry one, a protest. She was being sent to boarding school, and this was her bitter good-bye. What was the point of more babies? Why, she wondered, did they feel the need to replace her?

The note wasn't wrong. Children do find us out. Sooner or later they realize we are so much weaker, more flawed, and more scared than they ever imagined, even when they were imagining the worst. And they find out because they, too, become weak and flawed and scared, at least the lucky ones do. I suppose it's the best we can hope for. Even weak and flawed and scared, sometimes we do all right.

The girl intended to put a note under every hotel door, but she almost got caught (by Gudrun, of course) on the very first one. The girl threw the rest of the notes in the hotel dumpster. Some of them are still there, plastered to the bottom. The rest have made it to the landfill. Except for the one that escaped on the wind.

Maybe you've seen it?

# THE DEAD

Edward J. Arapian, a.k.a. the Sponge King, b. Constantinople,
May 1850, d. Key West, December 1920

For years, Arapian's wife, Harriet, had held a party, famous
throughout Key West, on his birthday. Then there was the
war, and nobody expected a party, except there were the invitations, embossed on thick cardstock, delivered three weeks
ahead of time, same as every other year. That was 1918, when
Arapian turned sixty-eight, two years before he died, seven
months before Harriet died.

In Key West, Arapian was known as the Turk, though he
was Armenian.

The extraction of fingernails; the application of burning
irons to the breast; the pinching of skin with burning clamps;
boiled butter poured into wounds; the tearing off of genitalia;

the penetration of orifices with swords, with brooms, with flesh; the sawing off of hands and feet, arms and legs; the bayoneting of babies; the slitting of throats, the exhibition of the massacred.

The difference between Turk and Armenian? The Turk extracted the Armenian's fingernails. The Turk applied burning irons to the Armenian's breast. The Turk pinched the skin of the Armenian with burning clamps. Or he had the Kurd do it.

Turkey for the Turks, they said.

In Key West, sponges made Arapian a millionaire, one of the richest men in America at the time, an immigrant from the Ottoman Empire, which would have killed him if it could.

Bow down to the almighty sponge! Either the highest order of plant or the lowest order of animal.

## A Brief History of Sponge Diving

In the beginning, there were naked divers, each weighed down by a marble stone. The divers cut sponges loose with knives held in their hands. They tucked those sponges into nets tied around their waists. From time to time, they wedged their marble stones into the mouths of sharks.

No tanks, no suits, just the air in their lungs.

But then in 1865, Fotis Mastoridis of Symi Island bought a diving suit and a helmet in Berlin. He convinced his fellow Greeks of the suit's safety by putting his pregnant wife inside and dropping her into the deep. Her feelings on the matter have not been recorded, but she surfaced unscathed, and the

Symians took to the new suits immediately. Other islanders quickly learned their ways.

Divers were to go down only twice a day, to spend only five minutes on the sea bottom, to rise slowly, to breathe slowly. With every exhalation, carbon dioxide filled their helmets. With every descent, nitrogen spread through their bodies, a martini hitting them at every ten meters. But money was to be made, houses to be paid for, debts to be honored, rules—as ever—to be broken in the name of commerce.

Ten thousand divers died and another twenty thousand were paralyzed. Each year only half the fleet returned.

Women dreamt nightly of their unburied husbands, dropped to the bottom of the sea or stashed in a pile of stones on an island where the only growth was a crop of small wooden crosses.

The diving suit was banned by the sultan's decree in 1881, but the ban was never enforced; it wasn't even written down. (The word of the sultan was supposed to be enough, but that worked only if you heard it.)

In the meanwhile, Symi grew rich, richer, richest. By 1900, it was the wealthiest port in the Mediterranean, a treasure of the Ottoman Empire, even if the empire was the enemy. Everyone on the island believed divers were rich, so the divers lived like the rich even during the months they were not paid. They imported luxuries from Istanbul; they built mansions; they adopted European dress. Then they dove in order to pay the debts they'd incurred—the nineteenth century's well-paid poor.

It was Greek sponges that Odysseus used to wipe up the blood of Penelope's suitors after he killed them. In Egypt, sponges wiped ink from papyrus. A vinegar-soaked sponge was stuffed in Jesus's mouth while he hung on the cross. In Paris, women dabbed their skin with the softest of sponges. But it was the industrial revolution—so much machinery to clean—that made the American market.

In Key West, the waters were not so deep. Sponges were retrieved from the side of a boat with a bucket and a hook. All you needed was a sculler to hold the boat steady while the sponger peered through his bucket's glass bottom, trying to calculate, through the water's shifting lens, where to plunge his hook. No helmets, no suits, no risk of the bends. They barely got wet.

In Key West, the sponge merchants—middlemen in suits of a different sort—grew wealthy, but the spongers did not.

Arapian had connections in Paris, in Constantinople, in London. The perfect middleman, the man who knew everybody, everywhere. He came to Key West on a tip, and there, in Key West, he found Harriet (her uncle had been the first to send a shipment of sponges to New York), and there, in Key West, he stayed.

Every day at three, there was a sponge auction on the docks, the harvest cleaned and sold and shipped. Every day Arapian bought and sold, never at a loss. Eventually he had boats of his own. Eventually nobody could outbid him. By the time the Greeks began diving the Gulf and stealing his market share, he was too old and too rich to be bothered. He had no loyalty to sponges, only to the men who had manned his boats, stocked his warehouse, shipped his wares. And he believed he was good to those men. They had fought him only once, over the unions; but he had long ago forgiven that lack of loyalty. Most of his men were dead already, anyhow; somehow he had outlived so many. At the time, Arapian thought he did not need forgiveness from the dead.

ARAPIAN'S BIRTHDAY PARTY was known as the Wonders of the Sea. Each year Harriet served a six-course dinner, each course featuring a local catch. No Key Wester was ever turned away, though an official invitation was a particular treasure.

*Harriet Ellen Kemp Arapian, b. Bahamas, August 1863, d. Key West, December 1918* (Actually 1909, but fiction must take some liberties.)

Harriet grew up in a house once floated on a barge from the Bahamas to Key West and furnished entirely with wrecker's treasure: a fan made of ivory and roseate spoonbill feathers, shipped from New Orleans, meant for Spain, wrecked on the Florida Reef; a telescope shipped from Spain, meant for New Orleans, wrecked on the Florida Reef; a full set of china shipped from England, meant for Havana (not a piece broken, though the boat went down); and so much more—a piano always slightly out of tune, a gold coin bearing the head of Athena, a rhinoceros horn, a brass birdcage, a wooden dollhouse, a ship's bell, a full wardrobe of French dresses, three Persian carpets, and a small gold cross, which Harriet wore around her neck her whole life. All wrecked on the Florida Reef.

Over the years, wrecking, sponging, cigar rolling, turtle hunting, and tourism made many Key Westers—the Kemps especially—rich, and yet the poor remained a never-ending resource, always replenished, just like the sea.

Harriet's insistence on holding Arapian's party in 1918 was because of the money she wanted to raise for Anahid.

*Anahid Restrepian, b. Ordu, December 1899, d. Los Angeles, February 1980*

The famous survivor of the Armenian Atrocities. Her book, full of daring escapes and terrible nightmares, was a best seller. Soon there would be a movie, in which Anahid reenacted her own suffering. For the past year, Anahid had appeared regularly at cities across the country, but she had yet to come to Florida, and Harriet had arranged for her to speak at the party, which was to be a fund-raiser for Armenian relief. Harriet, as her own death approached, was trying to shore up Arapian's chances for an afterlife.

**The Survivor**
*I was born in a killing station—Ordu, a port city on the Black Sea.*

From the time Anahid arrived in America, she was no longer a body in the world; she was a story. America's favorite suffering angel, 1917–1919.

*This saved the Turks the trouble of marching my family across the plains in the grand pretense of deportation.*

She gave speeches.

*It saved the Turks the trouble of putting my parents, my brothers, myself into cattle cars and shipping us to the place where we would be killed.*

She wrote a book.

*A ride we would have been obliged to buy tickets for, by the way.*

She starred in the movie of her own abuses—all under the instruction of the American couple who took her in, a Hollywood producer and his wife.

*Instead, my father and my three brothers were put on a boat. And they were taken out to sea and drowned.*

She delivered her speeches in English, a language she barely understood.

*Except I can't be sure, because I didn't see it happen. All my mother and I could be sure of was that they were taken to jail and they never came back.*

The speeches were written by a Hollywood scriptwriter, which does not mean they were untrue.

*My mother and I were bought by a Muslim man, who married us both. To protect us, he said.*

Anahid was turned into a story the way Daphne was transformed into a tree and Actaeon into a stag.

*I ask myself often, Should I tell my people's story or keep my people's secret?*

Sometimes she was the fairy-tale princess rescued from capture, other times a wrecked soul never really to be recovered.

*In the end, this man was able to protect me, but not my mother.*

No matter what story Anahid tried to tell, she was turned into another.

*"Pray for me," he said on our wedding day.*

She would come to recognize the false hope in the eyes of someone spotting a mirage.

*I ran away.*

And the last steps of someone already dead.

*I feel foolish for it; I didn't understand the things I would see.*

She came to recognize the crouch of someone checking for breath, for food, for shoes, for anything at all.

*Bodies were everywhere. You'd see a skirt hiked up, a shirt disarranged, and you'd want to fix it. But you were also repelled—the bodies are a horror, yet you want to love them, treat them with respect. But the bodies, they are monsters. You have never seen anything so disgusting. But sometimes it is your neighbor, your school friend, even your enemy and you want to love them . . .*

Women were prostituted to the Ottoman soldiers, until the women caught venereal diseases.

*If the soldiers knew we were rich, they put us in prison first, so that we'd bribe our way out.*

Women with venereal diseases were poisoned.

*They'd take our money over and over until we had none left. Then they killed us.*

The grasping actions of a falling empire.

*The gendarmes caught me. I was forced to walk with all the rest—toward the desert in Syria. Why they bothered with this pretense, I will never know. If we made it there, it was only to be killed.*

The sword saves bullets.

*Women tried to give their babies away.*

Women tried to give their babies away.

*For three lifetimes I walked.*

But we are on the way to a happy ending—a story written by another.

*At the beginning, a Turk bought me for eighty-five cents. For him, that was a good deal of money.*

*In the end, I was bought by an American missionary for a dollar.*

*That is how I came to America. That is how I was saved.*

*All of that suffering and I only grew in value.* Here her audiences would begin their applause. *Maybe I only grew in value by fifteen cents.* And here her audiences would rise to their feet. *But fifteen cents is something, isn't it?*

She was, it turned out, a very good performer.

Mrs. Vanderbilt herself suggested Harriet invite Anahid to Key West.

## The Sea of Wonders

In past years, Arapian's birthday party had been a full-service dinner for a hundred or more people under a tent, but when Arapian turned sixty-eight, in 1918, his birthday dinner was a buffet. The food was plentiful—war did not stop the sea from giving bounty. There were conch fritters, yellow turtle eggs, and turtle steaks, Bahamian conch salad scorchingly spiced, green turtle soup, crab gumbo, dolphin fillets, stone crabs, baked crawfish, mackerel, kingfish, and scallops. The food was endless. As if death would be kept at the door by gluttony. As if genocide could be countered by abundance. The guests couldn't stop remarking on it. And they couldn't help but notice, by way of contrast, how thin Harriet had become. How had they failed to notice until now?

She'd always been thin—long neck, long nose, spindle arms

and spindle legs (though those were rarely seen). All her life, Harriet was elegant or childlike, depending on how she chose to dress. Arapian was a shape-shifter too, able to perform European elegance or dockworker bravado as called upon. He had dressed to the hilt for the party—a tailored suit, polished shoes; his still thick, now white hair slicked back. Next to him, Harriet looked like a draped skeleton. People had to turn away or look her only in the eye.

At first they stood together in the living room, greeting guests as they arrived. Harriet was waiting for Anahid, and Arapian was waiting for the Greek, his old business partner, who had recently sent him a letter requesting a five-thousand-dollar settlement for an invention they had collaborated on.

But after an hour, neither Anahid nor the Greek had arrived. The house was swiftly filling, and the party spread into the small backyard and onto the large front porch. Harriet took a seat on the couch, with a lesser Vanderbilt down from New York next to her, while Arapian stood over them. Guests came to the couch in a swirling rotation. Already it was hard for Arapian to hear anything but the buzz and hum of the party; he and Harriet didn't even try to speak to each other. He knew they would talk later, after everyone had left.

Arapian's was a brick house with a tin roof—a house that couldn't be burned, to replace one that had. He hadn't felt the loss strongly—he didn't own mementos from his youth; he didn't treasure books or pianos the way Harriet did. He didn't care if people called him a Turk or an Armenian, a Greek or an American. He had what he needed to get what he wanted, which is to say, money. He wasn't a bad man, but he wasn't a fool, either; he knew how money had protected him and Harriet and their son, William, and he knew how if he was smart, it always could.

From the couch, Harriet and Arapian could see William through the window, no longer young, a little drunk and worrisome, out on the porch. Arapian had taken, in retirement, to writing long letters to William, full of instruction on the making of a man, letters he hand-delivered, but that neither of them ever discussed. The letters seemed to be having little effect, at least not a positive one.

Upstairs in a bathroom, refusing to come down and bear witness, was William's wife; their two children were asleep in Arapian and Harriet's bed—a problem to be solved later.

The living room was full of young men: navy men who'd been brought to the party by local girls, as well as the sons of Arapian's old friends and employees, most of them underemployed and eyeing the mainland, or underemployed and eyeing the navy. In the kitchen were their mothers, talking loudly, as if they didn't see each other most days. Their fathers were largely missing, most having died years ago, in what had felt like a sudden mass extinction. Only the Greek, not yet arrived, was left from the old days.

The Greek's father and his two uncles had been Symi divers mangled by the bends; none of them had lived to turn thirty. Still the Greek had followed them into the family business; and then he had followed the family business to Florida. He became Arapian's engineer, always looking for, and often finding, ways to improve the boats, the nets, the warehouse. Arapian liked to say that the Greek's ingenuity made him his fortune. Arapian liked, too, to say, that he had made the Greek.

They hadn't been close since they took opposite sides on the issue of the union, twenty years before, when Arapian threatened the men who tried to organize. But still the Greek's letter had come as a surprise, and Arapian had yet to answer it.

"I don't think he's coming," Arapian said loudly in Harriet's direction, and her response was to rise from the couch and go to the telephone to find out what had happened to Anahid.

At first Harriet had thought Anahid was simply running late, not so unusual given the sometime difficulties of traveling to Key West from the mainland, but when she called the hotel a nurse picked up and said Anahid was lying down a minute before setting out. She wasn't feeling well.

ANAHID HAD NOT been well for some time. How nice it would be if this story could present her as otherwise, but Anahid was in the midst of a complete emotional breakdown, perhaps brought on by wartime starvation, by rape, by the loss of her entire family, or maybe by the fact that she now lived in a country where she knew almost nobody, or by the fact that the American couple acting as her benefactors had become increasingly demanding and, in answer to Anahid's requests for a break in her touring, had begun referring to her contract, a document she had no memory of signing.

Remember, she was only nineteen.

At the time of Harriet's call, Anahid was lying stiffly atop her still-made hotel bed sobbing, holding the hand of her

Armenian-American translator, Lucintak, Lucy for short, a girl of seventeen who had been traveling with Anahid for the past month. The nurse who had answered the phone, Mrs. Brown, was an employee of Near East Relief, and Anahid's chaperone. She was trying to give Anahid a shot that might calm her.

The room felt damp. All of Key West felt damp, but inside the hotel room, the damp felt as if it had pooled in the corners, as if it clung to the walls and the carpet, and Mrs. Brown's skin.

"You will feel better outside, both of you will," Mrs. Brown said, as she tried to shift one girl aside in order to catch the then-flailing arm of the other. But the girls had wrapped each other in a tangle, and eventually Mrs. Brown gave up and crossed the room to sit in an armchair, also damp, and wait out the hysteria.

Mrs. Brown hadn't been east herself, but she had seen the photographs of orphan camps and starving women and deceased men. She understood that Anahid needed care, or at least rest, but she had also seen the response of the crowds when Anahid spoke. She had seen the donation receipts, and the shipments of food, medical supplies, and workers funded by those receipts, and she had decided the sacrifice of this one girl might well be acceptable in light of the greater cause. Mrs. Brown was a Christian woman and she believed in sacrifice.

After a time, the crying quieted, and the two girls became separate beings again, lying side by side—and as Mrs. Brown looked at them there on the small motel bed, how close they were in size and manner, she was the first to realize that Anahid did not always have to be the one to be Anahid.

"Get up," Mrs. Brown told Lucy, who looked at her with sudden alarm.

WHEN MRS. BROWN and Lucy arrived on Arapian's porch, Mrs. Brown ushered the girl past a bench full of uniformed navy boys, who barely had time to open their mouths before Mrs. Brown had Lucy safely inside. Immediately she and Lucy were surrounded by Arapian, Harriet, the lesser Vanderbilt, and two local girls Harriet had hired to help out. Each seemed to be trying to force a drink into their hands, and Lucy shrank against the side of Mrs. Brown, who automatically wrapped an arm around her shoulder.

"We're so glad you were able to make it. You look much recovered," Harriet said, first to the shrinking girl and then to Mrs. Brown, who unexpectedly found herself holding a plate piled with conch fritters, yellow turtle eggs, and a tiny turtle steak.

"Yes, of course," Mrs. Brown said with a glance at Lucy, who took a deep breath.

"I'm so glad to meet you," Harriet said softly as she clasped Lucy's hand in both of hers. "This is my husband, Edward," she said, gesturing to Arapian, who in response took a step back, and out of the orbit of Harriet's arm, which tried to draw him in closer. His retreat had been in response to the stern manner of Mrs. Brown rather than out of reluctance to meet the pretty young girl in front of him, but still he did not step forward again. He had forgotten how tired these parties made him.

"Hello," Lucy said, remembering to speak Armenian, as Mrs. Brown had instructed. Arapian took another step back. "Thank you for your hospitality."

Mrs. Brown squeezed Lucy about her shoulders, and Lucy said, "Thank you for helping our people," this time directly to Arapian, who took yet another step back. His steady retreat had become so noticeable that Mrs. Brown actually took a step forward, drawing Lucy, who was under her arm, and Harriet, who still held Lucy by one hand, along with her. The four of them were so close to a serving table piled with food that Arapian accidentally brushed his hand against a pile of buttered shrimp. He held his greasy hand out to the side, careful not to touch his suit.

"Oh dear," he said, a smile engulfing his face, as everyone turned their eyes from his hand to him. "I've always been nervous around young ladies." He looked to Harriet as if for affirmation, but the expression on her face did not serve his purposes, and so he changed tack. "It's been a long time since I heard the language of my parents," he said in Armenian, to Lucy. "I'm sorry for your suffering," he added, and Harriet and Mrs. Brown both nodded as if in approval, though neither understood what he'd said. Lucy looked at her feet.

I have to be Anahid, she thought. Lucy, too, had seen the donations and the photos of orphan camps that Mrs. Brown had seen. I must do the things Anahid would do, and yield the same results, she thought.

AT THE HOTEL, alone at last in a quiet room, Anahid sank deeper and deeper into her bed. She felt the balmy air through the window Mrs. Brown had left open in an attempt to combat the damp. In the distance, she could hear the sounds of people talking—the party she was missing, perhaps. A sound that made her room seem more silent.

Anahid's despair spread over the room's silence. Alone and quiet, alone and quiet, the very things she had wanted, yet she sank deeper and deeper.

What to say here? How can you expect me to know her suffering!

Each night for 379 nights, Anahid had taken the shadow that filled her each day, and folded it and folded it and folded it until it became a tiny black seed inside her, which she delicately coughed into her hand. Each night, so that she could sleep, she placed that black seed in a glass cup she kept by her bedside. Each morning, she tipped the seed back into her palm and swallowed it, where inside of her it unfolded and unfolded and unfolded, so that once again it became the whole of her, and she began again the process of refolding it and refolding it and refolding it, so that it wasn't the whole of her.

But that night, try as she could to contain it, Anahid felt the shadow spread across her skin, covering her nails and her hair and every inch of her. Alone and quiet was no cure. She got out of bed, left the hotel, and walked toward the sound of the party.

LUCY HAD HER FIRST DRINK——ever——at Arapian's party: a glass of champagne that appeared in her hand while people were asking her questions——it was surprising how free people felt to ask her questions——and at some point she found herself separate from Mrs. Brown, out on the porch, speaking entirely in English, flirting with sailors, and laughing as if she had never heard of suffering. Lucy did not feel she had stopped being Anahid; instead she had become the Anahid she wanted Anahid to be. Why couldn't Anahid forget all she had been through and be happy?

Besides, wasn't Lucy also a survivor? Hadn't her parents had the good sense and the good fortune to leave the Ottoman Empire years before the atrocities—as Arapian himself had—and didn't that give all three of them—Anahid, Arapian, and Lucy—reason to be happy? Lucy resolved to stop crying with Anahid, to stop embracing Anahid's pain and trying to absorb Anahid's story; instead she would teach Anahid to be an American, to start over and lift herself up—to be happy.

It was as Lucy reached this conclusion that Arapian saw her through the window, laughing on the porch of his sturdy home, and he felt pride at the resilience of her spirit, he felt a sense of accomplishment, as if somehow by bringing her to his house he had been the one to save her.

FROM THE STREET, Anahid also saw Lucy laughing.

How young she was.

Anahid had a long history of laughing, of course, but long histories sometimes have abrupt endings.

"You'll recover," Anahid told herself in the voice of her benefactor. "You're young," she told herself in the voice of Mrs. Brown, and then in that of her benefactor's wife. You're young you're young you're young. Just then Lucy caught Anahid's eye and abruptly froze, but Anahid put a finger to her lips and gave a soft smile.

Lucy started to move toward Anahid, who was on the porch steps then, but Anahid quickly shook her head, and Lucy stopped, frozen again, while the men and women all around her kept laughing and talking.

Anahid slipped into the party quiet as she could. Right away, she was handed a glass of champagne by a girl who looked run off her feet—it was just time for the toast.

Arapian, though Anahid did not know that name or anything, really, of this party she had been asked to attend, was at the center of the living room, in his fine suit, waving his now clean hands, calling out, "Gather round, everyone, gather round."

"Anahid," he called out loudly—to Lucy on the porch, of course, but Anahid shrank slowly into herself anyway. She had learned to project invisibility.

Lucy came slowly in through the front door with all the denizens of the porch crowding behind her. If she'd stopped, they would have surged ahead, knocking her over. She sought Anahid out with her eyes, but Anahid gave another tiny shake of her head, and Lucy looked away. Soon Mrs. Brown appeared beside Lucy, her eyes even wider than Lucy's at the sight of Anahid stock-still in the middle of the living room in what appeared to be her nightgown.

"I'm so grateful to you all," Arapian began once Lucy and Mrs. Brown were beside him, "for gathering to celebrate my birthday. As you know, it is my wife, Harriet, who does the work for this party, so first, as always, we toast her." At that, the majority of party guests raised their glasses—a ritual with which they were familiar.

"And," Arapian continued, "I raise my glass to God, who has granted me another year, and I raise my glass to all of you who have made Key West my only home—"

At this, the Greek came in the door.

"Especially to you, old friend," Arapian said smoothly. The Greek nodded, perhaps begrudgingly but in accordance with old times. He had learned that Arapian paid his friends, never his enemies, and the Greek had grown old without growing rich.

"Tonight," Arapian continued, "I will not give my usual speech but will instead turn the floor over to our special guest, Anahid Restrepian, who has found refuge and safety in our great country, and who is here to ask for your support for those who have not found refuge or safety. A pretty girl like her," Arapian said, and here he paused as if he had lost his thought, "she deserves our attention."

"Speech," Arapian called out suddenly, and the whole room, including Anahid, turned to Lucy. Lucy gulped visibly, and the real Anahid put a hand to her face and, behind it, smiled.

MRS. BROWN HAD TOLD Lucy to speak only in Armenian, and very little at that, but what with the champagne, with the sudden embarrassment of being placed at the center of the crowd, and with the responsibility of having to speak for Anahid in front of Anahid, the poor girl panicked.

"I don't know what to say," she said in English.

"No," Arapian said, "it is we who don't know what to say. It is we who cannot imagine what it would be like to be in your shoes. You must tell us."

He spread his arms then, and smiled, in a way that suggested he had no idea of the world. And then, perhaps Lucy did feel like Anahid. She looked directly at Arapian and started. "If you were in my shoes," she said, "you would have been arrested and then killed because you were thought too old for the labor battalions—which is where your son would have been sent." She looked at William, irreparably drunk and sprawled next to his mother, who sat ramrod straight on the couch. "Your son would have been forced to construct the railroads, which would then be used to transport other Armenians to towns where they could be more conveniently killed. His children, your grandchildren, would have been told to march—with or without their mother"—Lucy looked at Arapian's daughter-in-law, perched on the stairs, only halfway down from her hide-out in the bathroom—"who probably would have been killed or raped sometime earlier." At that, the daughter-in-law fled back upstairs, and Lucy turned back to Arapian. "Your grand-children would have marched until they fell, dead of starva-tion, or until they froze in the night, or until they had their heads bashed in by a soldier who had suddenly grown irritated at the sight of them."

The Greek stepped toward her then, perhaps to stop her, but Arapian reached out and grabbed the Greek's shoulder, clutched it, his fingers pressing deep into his friend's soft flesh. Arapian had had a sister once. She had stayed behind, in Con-stantinople, with their parents.

"Or maybe you"—Lucy looked at Arapian, then William, then Harriet, then all around the room—"maybe you would have been one of the lucky ones who slipped away, who found a cave to hide in, or a sympathetic family to shelter with." She paused. "But probably not. Probably you wouldn't have been as lucky as you think you are. Or maybe your grandson would

be one of the orphans—unsure what happened to the rest
of you—"

It was Anahid who stopped her. Anahid who put a hand on
her arm, as good as putting it over Lucy's mouth.

The seed folded and unfolded inside of her.

The two girls stood in the center of the room, at the center
of the room's attention.

"Maybe," Harriet said, slowly rising from the couch, then
turning to Mrs. Brown, who had stepped close to her girls still
holding the full plate of food she had never felt comfortable
eating or putting down, "you ought to take Anahid home now."

"Yes, of course," Mrs. Brown said, handing the plate off to
Harriet, with an odd smile.

It was, Mrs. Brown would think later, one of the proudest
moments of her life, though why she should lay any claim to it,
she really didn't know.

As Lucy and Mrs. Brown stepped out the door, Anahid
trailed after them without a word.

NOT MANY GUESTS stayed long after that, though most of them
made any number of donations and pledges. A few tried to
make remarks about the ways of teenagers and foreigners; William offered a stirring defense of Lucy/Anahid's spirit, but by
then everybody was too embarrassed by his behavior to listen
to him.

Neither Arapian nor Harriet said anything about the toast
or Anahid. They seemed to give up on their charitable effort
the moment the women went out the door. They accepted the

money that was handed to them with generous thanks, but nothing more. At the end of the night, they passed the donations on to the lesser Vanderbilt, who would deliver them to New York.

Eventually they found themselves alone on the porch, the position they had taken after every party thrown in their house since it was built. William and his wife were upstairs, engaged in a hushed argument meant not to wake their sleeping children; the two local girls were in the kitchen cleaning up; and everyone else had gone home or gone to continue the party elsewhere.

"Did I ever tell you about the woman who was my nanny?" Harriet asked.

Arapian shook his head. How moved he had been when he'd first met Harriet. This serious young girl who wanted so much to talk to him, who was so overjoyed to see him whenever they met.

"She was an obeah woman."

"In Nassau," Arapian said.

Harriet's great-grandparents had fled the Americas when the Revolution began. Like so many Tories, they took refuge in the Bahamas, where they profited, until they found their way to Key West, where they profited even more.

"She took care of me when I was very little. She used to give me medicines without telling my parents."

"How can you remember that?" Arapian said with a laugh. "You were just a baby."

"She was tremendously tall," Harriet said.

"To a baby," Arapian teased, but Harriet refused to respond in kind.

"She was taller than my father; I know that much." Harriet paused. "She told me once how to kill a person."

Arapian waited. Sometimes he misheard things.

"All you have to do is wish them dead," Harriet said. "You can kill someone by wishing them dead."

Arapian stayed quiet. He did not want the night to end this way. He wanted Harriet to be pleased with her success.

"I'm very tired," Harriet said. "I'm ready, you know."

How he wanted her to look at him then and smile. How he wanted, one more time, to feel desire pass between them—that unacknowledged friend of theirs which had gone missing in recent years.

"I want you to know that," Harriet said, as she stood and turned to enter the house. "I'm okay with what you wish."

But this last remark was so in line with how Harriet always was, her usual accommodations, that Arapian failed to notice what she was asking, and one more chance for generosity passed him by.

WHEN ARAPIAN DIED, two years later, he left half of his money to Near East Relief, a fact that gave his son very complicated feelings of bitterness, anger, and shame. His cause of death was lung cancer, though Arapian never knew it. A cancer probably brought on by the constant cigars he and his men smoked to cover up the terrible smell of the sponges, which, after all, were living creatures beaten to death with clubs before they were bleached.

Lucy never forgot Anahid, of course; but she did not stay on with her. Lucy went back to her family in New York, she found

work in a factory, she married a boy who was too young for
the first war but not too old for the second, which he did not
survive. Lucy became a nurse then, after that.

When Anahid's movie, *An Armenian Girl,* came out, just a
year after the events in Key West, Lucy saw it with her parents
and her sisters, who treated Lucy as if she herself were the star.

Lucy tried every chance she got to tell Anahid's story. For
years she raised money for the orphans from her friends and
coworkers, who gave what they could, not because of the
orphans but because they cared for Lucy.

As to Anahid—her strange story was not yet over. After
the great success of *An Armenian Girl,* her benefactors decided
the necessary sequel was for Anahid to save a child. So they
adopted an Armenian orphan as a gift for her, for her to raise.
But this, Anahid was sure, was not in any contract she had ever
signed. On the day of the arrival of the orphan, Aram, Anahid
could not be raised from the four-poster bed provided for her
by her benefactors. Her eyes were open but her mind clearly
closed. When Mrs. Brown lifted Anahid's arm, it dropped.
When Mrs. Brown lightly slapped Anahid's cheeks—what
choice did she have?—Anahid did not respond.

Many attempts were made to wake her, most regularly by
placing the young Aram on her bed, but none succeeded until
finally Anahid was moved to a hospital and the whole orphan
endeavor was dropped. There was some discussion afterward
if Aram could be placed elsewhere, but in the end Anahid's
benefactors were not so cruel; they took him in and spoiled
him just as they had their other children.

Anahid was the only thing Aram remembered of those early years. Lucky him.

What sights he had seen by then. What sensations he had felt. Thirst, hunger, seasickness—but all he remembered was a fairy tale come to life: Sleeping Beauty in her bed waiting for the proper kiss.

Eventually Anahid moved on her own to Los Angeles, where she worked for a film studio, though it never suited her. In the end, she found work as a photographer—family portraits mostly. She died in 1980 in California.

Sometimes she was happy, sometimes she wasn't. She married, she had children, she did not hide her story, nor did she tell it.

Indeed, for all of Anahid's years in America—more than sixty—she thought the Turkish government might still track her down and kill her.

Silence was so important to the Turks, more so every year. But Anahid never understood why.

Even she, the one who lived her story, sought ways not to believe it.

IN THE END, nobody remembered much of Arapian's party, not with the darker consequences of the war still to come, the terrible downturn in nearly everyone's economic circumstances. People would remember the starving Armenians, but more as a chastisement to eat their own dinners than to sacrifice those dinners on the Armenians' behalf. If any of the guests saw the movie made of Anahid's life, which raised a million dollars for

Near East Relief, they never noticed that the girl who was the star was not the girl who spoke at the party.

What people remembered was how thin Harriet was, how long she lingered in her illness, how difficult it became for her, and how grateful they felt not to be in her circumstances. That and the food.

# AN OTTOMAN'S ARABESQUE

>>>————————————————————>

His eyes were frequently inflamed and he feared going blind.

Most of the time he wore blue glasses. The papers often mentioned them, in a joking sort of way. The papers found him comic, it seems.

He was born in Egypt to Turkish parents (very rich), studied in Paris (at an Egyptian school), and became an Ottoman ambassador: to Athens, to St. Petersburg, to Vienna. A servant to the sultan most of his life.

But from 1865 to 1868, he lived in a palatial Parisian apartment, and for three years, he bought paintings and he gambled, and at the end of those three years, he sold all of his paintings and paid all of his debts. He was thirty-seven years old.

History would declare many of the paintings masterpieces. There were more than a hundred by the likes of Courbet, Ingres, Rousseau, Meissonier, Corot, and Delacroix. But how would history remember him? Not as Khalil Bey, diplomat, a man who helped negotiate the treaty that ended the Crimean War and a liberal reformer of the empire, nor as Khalil Bey, patron, among the first to collect many of the nineteenth century's most celebrated painters, but as Khalil Bey, the world's most notorious collector of the world's most notorious collection of erotic art.

*The Odalisque*

JEAN-AUGUSTE-DOMINIQUE INGRES

1814

OIL ON CANVAS

35" × 64"

Like so many great beauties, she is something of a freak, painted with extra vertebrae in her back, so many that should she have tried to step out of her frame, she would have bent to the ground, where she could only have slid along the floor, serpentlike, unable to stand.

Also, her left arm is shorter than her right.

When French critics condemned the painting, Ingres, who was temporarily in Rome, swore never to return to Paris, where, inconveniently, his fiancée was a resident. The engagement was broken, and Ingres, on the strength of a written correspondence and the recommendation of his friends, proposed to Madeleine Chapelle, a woman he had never seen, also a resident of Paris, though, conveniently, willing to relocate.

Ingres modeled the Odalisque on Jacques-Louis David's unfinished *Portrait of Madame Récamier,* who, dressed as a vestal virgin, reclines casually on a sofa. Vestal virgins had been Rome's priestesses, responsible for maintaining the city's eternal fire. They could free slaves by touching them and pardon criminals sentenced to death by looking at them. And they got front-row seats at sporting competitions. Each vestal virgin took a thirty-year vow of celibacy, after which she had the option to marry. Some men believed marrying a vestal virgin would cure them of disease or pardon their sins or grant them eternal life. But after their thirty years, most vestal virgins opted not to marry at all.

At age fifteen, Madame Récamier, the subject of Jacques-Louis David's unfinished portrait, had been married to a man nearly thirty years her senior, generally believed to have been her biological father. It is rumored he married her not out of some perverse sexual desire, but to ensure she would become his heir. Unfortunately, before his death, he lost the bulk of his once considerable fortune.

In Turkish, *odalik* means "chambermaid," and though many think odalisques were the women among whom sultans romped, in reality, they served those who served the sultan. They were slaves who tended the other women of the harem: the concubines, who were under the wives, and the wives, who were under the sultana valide, the sultan's mother. The sultana valide was often the most powerful person in the seraglio, the living quarters of the harem. Sometimes she was more powerful than the sultan himself, who, after all, was sometimes just a child.

The sultana valide was frequently the largest landowner in the empire; often she would own entire villages. Throughout history the sultanas constructed mosques, hospitals, public baths, eateries for the poor, schools, libraries, fountains, and other monuments, paying not only for the construction of each of these sites but creating endowments to maintain and manage them.

When Ingres painted his Odalisque, it was rumored that the sultana valide, Nakşidil Sultan, was actually Aimée du Buc de Rivéry, Josephine Bonaparte's cousin, who as a girl had been traveling from Martinique to a convent school in France when her ship was boarded by pirates, who sold her into slavery. But, in fact, this was not the case. It is, however, true that Nakşidil Sultan had a great love of France and did her best to bring the harem into a more modern age, taking the harem women on picnics and boating trips. Before each such excursion, colorful silk tunnels were extended from the doorways of the seraglio to allow the women to board their carriages unseen. The mere sight of these silk tunnels caused some men to faint.

Many scenes from the seraglio would be immortalized by a Turkish painter with Greek origins, Osman Hamdi Bey, who was also an esteemed archaeologist. During the three years of Khalil Bey's collecting, Osman Hamdi Bey was a student in Paris, and so it is possible that he visited Khalil Bey's remarkable apartment with one of his teachers, the artist Jean-Léon Gérôme, whose work Khalil Bey also owned. Osman Hamdi Bey's most famous painting, *The Tortoise Trainer,* depicted the eighteenth-century Ottoman practice of affixing candles to tortoises' backs so that during nighttime parties they could wander the seraglio gardens, lighting them. Long after Osman Hamdi Bey's death, *The Tortoise Trainer* would sell for more than three million dollars. Most of Osman Hamdi Bey's paintings are considered a rebuttal to Western orientalism, as they include scenes of Islamic scholars arguing interpretations of the Koran and women standing up doing their housework, as opposed to lying down in a drug-induced haze.

Though Ingres's Odalisque lies on her sofa in much the same position as Jacques-Louis David's Madame Récamier, the Odalisque has been undressed. Her back is to us, though she's turned her neck so as to look us in the eye, and she is naked except for the gold scarf wound about her head. All around her are sumptuous fabrics: blue satin, fur, peacock feathers gathered into a fan. At her feet is an opium pipe.

This, too, is how history has painted Khalil Bey: rounded and soft, with an opium pipe at his feet.

Sometimes, in the midst of a card game, Khalil Bey would close his eyes to ease their inflammation. The other players often mistook this for some sign and would decrease or increase their bidding accordingly.

Ingres's Odalisque was commissioned by Caroline Murat, Emperor Napoleon's sister and queen of Naples and, perhaps not incidentally, a friend to Madame Récamier. Unfortunately, on account of Napoleon's defeat at Waterloo, and Caroline Murat's husband's subsequent execution, and her own desperate flight from Naples to Austria in order to avoid the same fate, she never paid for the work.

For a while afterward, Ingres made his living in Rome drawing pencil portraits of tourists, a lucrative practice that filled him with despair.

Sometimes Khalil Bey stood across the room from his Odalisque and stared at her. Sometimes he walked casually past her and then with a sudden leap turned to catch her in a new position, which, of course, he never did. Whenever he looked at the Odalisque, he felt an impulse to turn, like her, and glance over his shoulder. Sometimes he would. Sometimes, instead, he took pleasure in his ownership and ran his finger down the long curving lines of her painted body, imagining that, with his touch, he was the one to create her. Once he pressed the tip of his tongue against the small strokes of her eyelashes.

There is much the Odalisque leaves to the viewer's imagination. Who is she, what has she been up to, and, most significantly, what is she looking at? Has she cast her eyes over her shoulder to watch the artist in the act of creation? Or is this an invitation to something riskier? Hasn't myth taught us it is a danger to look? Is she the danger, or is she courting it? Is the Odalisque looking at us, here in the future, or is she looking backward into some moment of her own history?

There is only one story of a slave girl escaping the harem. (Had she waited nine years she would have been released, but probably she had her reasons for not.) She escaped, in the night, as far as the Janissary Court, where, panicking at the guarded gates, she climbed an enormous tree that stood above two small columns on which decapitations were carried out.

The only way in, or out, of the harem was through a door of iron and a door of brass. Inside the harem, the door of iron was guarded by the eunuchs; outside the harem, the door of brass was guarded by the woodcutters. The eunuchs kept the women in; the woodcutters kept all others out. One responsibility of the woodcutters was cutting wood, but they also made up one of the fiercest detachments of the Ottoman army.

From her tree, the girl could see the dormitories of the wood-cutters; the private stables of the sultan, where his favorite horses were kept; the Gate of the Departed, where the dead exited; and the Gate of Felicity, where the living entered. She could also see the woodcutter guards who when she passed had been asleep on their feet, or so it seemed.

She stayed in her tree for three days. She could see so much from there, without being seen—or so it seemed.

In fact, the woodcutters had watched her from the beginning. They did not wish to admit, one to the other, that they had seen her; they all knew what the consequence would be. What they wished for was to each slip looks up into the tree, to glance repeatedly at the forbidden harem girl.

But eventually hunger overtook the girl, or maybe fear, and she jumped, or maybe fell, striking her head on one of the marble columns on her way down. And so she died. One of the woodcutters covered her face, and another smuggled her out, though not through the Gate of the Departed, where he would be seen and all discovered. As a result, the girl is said to have never truly left the harem; it is said that she is there still.

*The Turkish Bath*

JEAN-AUGUSTE-DOMINIQUE INGRES

1862

OIL ON CANVAS ON WOOD PANEL

43" × 43"

Ingres first painted *The Turkish Bath* in 1859 as a rectangle but a year later revised it to a circle. This was, it is said, to cut out the body of the woman in the bottom right-hand quadrant, who was "too clearly in ecstasy." Even without her, *The Turkish Bath* was considered so indecent that it wasn't shown in public until 1905, more than forty years after it was painted. It was then that Picasso became a fan. Degas championed it as well, though the writer Paul Claudel called it a "cake full of maggots" and the Louvre turned it down twice, until the Germans expressed interest.

In the *Bath,* women are layered on women, naked and lounging, arms over their heads, hands on each other's breasts, limbs splayed out, their faces expressing desire, languor, and, in at least one case, an irritated boredom.

The painting is generally considered an arabesque, in which the repetition of a geometric form suggests the infinite repetition of that form. In Islamic art, that repetition is meant to remind us of the infinite extension of God. In *The Turkish Bath,* it suggests an infinity of women and a peephole through which to view them.

Harem women would often sit at latticed windows and look out; there they could see without being seen.

Critics like to call Ingres's lines serpentine. In one study for *The Turkish Bath* there is a woman with three arms. It is not such a difficult mistake to imagine when you view the painting, woman blurring into woman as they sit, entwined, blank-minded and blissed out, after the steam of the bath.

When he learned the roman alphabet, there was no letter Khalil Bey loved more than the letter *S*.

The heated portion of the bath is known as the tepidarium. There women could rest and drink coffee or eat sherbet. Talk.

Sing. Listen. Sleep. This most likely is what *The Turkish Bath* depicts.

In the 1850s, an Englishman opened what he called a Turkish bath attached to his house and began claiming the bath could cure toothache, rheumatism, gout, and syphilis.

It was rumored Khalil Bey moved to Paris to undergo treatment for syphilis, which he was said to have caught in St. Petersburg. At the time, some men considered syphilis a rite that marked their passage from boyhood to manhood; some men boasted of it.

Khalil Bey kept his condition to himself, as he kept much of himself to himself, though this particular discretion was not to the advantage of his lovers. It was rumored he caught the disease because his bad eyesight prevented him from noticing the symptoms in a past lover. Perhaps, but probably not, given his eye for the female form.

Syphilis wasn't actually called syphilis until the sixteenth century, when an Italian physician, Girolamo Fracastoro, wrote an epic poem about a shepherd boy named Syphilus who defied the sun god Apollo, then became ill. Before Fracastoro's poem, syphilis was often called "the French disease," though the French called it "the Italian disease," the Dutch called it "the Spanish disease," the Russians called it "the Polish disease," and Tahitians called it "the British disease." Turks called it "the Christian disease."

Turkish baths were modeled on Roman baths. During the Middle Ages, European men and women stayed in their baths so long they sometimes ate whole meals on tables that floated in front of them. In Islam, if water is not available for ritual cleansing, dust or dirt can be used instead. In the Turkish bath, one starts first in a warm room, then moves to a hot room, then lounges, post-cleansing, in a cool room, where entertainment and food are often provided. In the women's bath, girls were sometimes discreetly displayed and their marriages negotiated. The women of the harem often spent large portions of their day in the bath, talking and napping and eating. But they never sat in tubs of water, what we might think of as a bath, as still water was believed to be unclean, a repository for evil spirits.

Besides, the harem had a history of drownings.

In the seventeenth century, Sultan Ibrahim is said to have had his entire harem, 280 women, sewn into weighted sacks and cast into the Bosporus. A passing ship found one concubine, who claimed to have swum free when her sack came untied. A sailor was quickly sent diving to the Bosporus's bottom, where he supposedly found hundreds of sacks standing upright, some with head and hair floating free, like strange underwater blossoms.

They were the most beautiful women he had ever seen. He could not stop himself. He took the closest by the hair, pulled her to him, and pressed his lips fervently to hers. The sirens almost took me, he would say later, trying to make a joke of it.

Prior to becoming sultan, Ibrahim had been kept in quarters known as "the Cage" for twenty-two years, ostensibly to protect him from assassination, but more likely to prevent his plotting the assassination of his brother, the then sultan. It is assumed that this incarceration drove him insane, and that much of his behavior is explained by his insanity.

Eventually Ibrahim's own army had him killed. Ibrahim's six-year-old son, Mehmed IV became sultan.

It is strange, though, that the story of Ibrahim drowning his harem came out only after his assassination. It is possible the story was created to undermine the surprising posthumous popularity of the supposed madman.

The Ottomans understood well the value of rumors.

Khalil Bey, too, understood that his reputation mattered more than his reality. Still, he made a point of never lying. The key to diplomacy is being known for telling the truth.

In the end, the concubine allegedly rescued from the bottom of the Bosporus was taken to Paris, where she became quite a sensation.

Ingres was eighty-two when he finished *The Turkish Bath*.

It is a history of Ingres's imagination. An original built of echoes. He didn't use a single live model to paint it. It is a painting of other paintings. Ingres's wife, Madeleine Chapelle, dead ten years by then, is at the front with her arms over her head. The guitar player with her back turned is a near copy of Ingres's painting *The Bather of Valpinçon*. The Odalisque is there in the bath, not aged a day despite the passage of more than forty years. The face of one woman in particular is repeated over and over, but in different attitudes—angry, bored, ecstatic, desperate, satisfied, mischievous. The infinite nature of a single woman ripples across the room.

In the harem, women were prisoners, and yet so many of them cried the day they were freed. In 1909, when the empire was in its final dissolve and the sultan had gone into exile, messages were sent to villages all across the Anatolian plains and up into the mountains. Any family who had lost or sold a girl to the seraglio could reclaim her. On the appointed day, the women of the harem lined the assembly hall, and the men of their families, some unseen for decades, some unknown entirely, were admitted. At a signal, the collection of harem women lifted their veils, and a collective gasp went up from the collection of village men. Was it surprise at their beauty? Surprise at their lack of it? Who can say what they saw?

Fathers struggled to recognize their daughters grown old, brothers learned that their sisters had died in the intervening years, cousins who had never met went home together. Other men left as they came, without even news of their lost girls. And then there were the women who stood waiting, unclaimed. Local homes had to be found for them, and at times in the years after, they could be seen in the city, their well-trained grace still evident beneath the draped folds of their faded finery.

Khalil Bey left home at the age of nine, and one could say he never truly returned. The empire had many such sons, but few with his influence. Periodically the sultan would fire him for some offense, but always he took him back.

*Sleep*

GUSTAVE COURBET

1866

OIL ON CANVAS

$53\frac{1}{8}'' \times 78\frac{3}{4}''$

Imagine that apartment, the paintings hung ten to a wall. A single painting could leave Khalil Bey speechless; imagine the effect of a hundred. He was overcome five times a day, though he did his best not to show it.

He was in love with so many things. Sometimes he did not go home for days and then for days more he would not leave home. The buildings, the bohemians, the corrupt politicians and the noble ones, the cultured women and the whores, he loved them all. He could not seem to see reality without transforming it into something both melancholy and joyous.

"When you wear glasses you are accustomed to seeing everything through a frame," he joked. "The world is nothing more than a museum to me."

During his three years in Paris, Khalil Bey's primary mistress was Jeanne de Tourbey, a Frenchwoman who had previously been mistress to Prince Napoleon, the emperor's cousin, who, at the time, had put her on an improving regimen, hiring a tutor to introduce her to writers and musicians and artists, all of whom she later introduced to Khalil Bey. Among those cultural aristocrats was the controversial but popular painter Gustave Courbet.

When Courbet's *A Burial at Ornans,* which depicted an ordinary village funeral in the scale of a historic battle, was exhibited in Frankfurt in 1852, it generated so many arguments as to its quality that cafés posted signs banning discussion of Courbet or his paintings.

Courbet's *The Stone Breakers* shocked audiences because one man had a broken shoe and the other patched trousers.

Courbet's *The Bathers* was criticized not only for the size of the nude bather's buttocks but the dirtiness of her feet. One critic offered five hundred francs to anyone who could "throw her down," and Napoleon III was rumored to have swatted her backside with his riding crop. This last rumor was perpetuated most of all by Courbet himself, who reacted to the story first with fury and then with delight, as if he had been spanked and had then found, after his anger, that he liked it.

Until Courbet, nudes were unrecognizable: their skin glossed, their faces smoothed. But when, in a commission for Khalil Bey, Courbet painted two women, life size, in bed, more naked than nude, one was clearly Jo Hiffernan, the long-time lover of James Whistler, who was himself a protégé and friend of Courbet's.

Whistler was outraged, though he staked his anger on artistic grounds. "Courbet and his influence was disgusting!" he wrote sometime later. "The regret I feel and the rage, hate, even. . . . It's not poor Courbet whom I find repugnant, any more than his work . . . it's that damned realism. . . . Ah! How I wish I had been a pupil of Ingres."

Ingres: the idealist. Courbet: the realist. And which was Khalil Bey?

"Beauty is real," he liked to say. Or sometimes, "What's real is beauty." The whole world, to Khalil Bey, seemed an exaggeration beyond belief.

Yet as a gambler, he was known for meeting great wins with the same cool face with which he met great losses.

When Khalil Bey first visited Courbet's studio, in the company of Jeanne de Tourbey, he tried to purchase *Venus Pursuing Psyche in Her Jealousy*, a painting of the goddess looming over the sleeping mortal, her jealousy provoked by the mortal's beauty. But the painting had been promised to another, who unscrupulously offered to sell it to Khalil Bey for a profit; Khalil Bey, recognizing that the money would not go to Courbet, refused. This pleased Courbet, who offered to paint a second work, a sequel. This became *Sleep*.

The women in *Sleep* have their eyes closed but they do not look as if they are sleeping. One has her leg hooked over the other, whose lips are pursed just above her companion's breast, as if she is blowing gently upon it, or about to bestow a kiss.

They are naked now, just as they were then.

How did Khalil Bey see *Sleep*? Were the female lovers nothing more than a catalyst for his erotic imagination? Couldn't such a thing have been bought more cheaply? It was rumored he, too, had an affair with Jo Hiffernan, Whistler's and then Courbet's model. Perhaps this added to poor Whistler's jealousy.

"I am memorizing beauty," Khalil Bey would often say when he was alone with a woman and staring at her. It was a line, but also true.

He liked especially to stand with the real Jo beside him and the Sleepers in front of him, so he could turn from one to the other. Ever the diplomat, he offered once to try to mend Jo's break with Whistler, with whom she had a little boy, but she declined.

Ottomans, by the way, believed all children to be legitimate, regardless of the married or unmarried state of their parents.

Several of Whistler's most famous paintings are of Jo. But there is one, *Harmony in Blue and Silver,* in which a small full-length figure, a man with his back to the viewer, faces out to sea, nearly fading into the sandy shore, which dwarfs him. It is Courbet.

Over the years, Courbet painted four portraits of Jo. One he kept in his possession his entire life, including during his exile in Switzerland after he was imprisoned for the politics he had once been celebrated for. The same Courbet, who once said, "My love does not go so far as a trip with a woman. Knowing that there are women everywhere in the world, I see no point in dragging one with me." The same Courbet who wrote one former mistress demanding that she return two portraits he had painted of her. "Or," he wrote, "destroy them yourself before a witness and then I will pay [you] for the use that I had of your body for a year." (She had offended Courbet by bringing her new lover along to the train station to see Courbet off—after Courbet refused to bring her on his trip.)

In an early version of *Venus Pursuing Psyche in Her Jealousy,* the painting Khalil Bey first tried to buy, Courbet sketched himself asleep, in the position where Psyche now lies. The goddess was intended to loom over him. In another painting, *The Wounded Man,* Courbet painted himself reclining, with his eyes closed, a red stain on his chest where he has been stabbed. In an earlier version, Courbet lay in bed next to a woman. She was replaced by his wound. The truth was, Courbet had trouble painting men and women together.

According to the French papers, when Khalil Bey wanted to seduce a woman, he would buy her a tea set. Supposedly he had a man on hire to supply him with tea sets. But when someone owned the paintings Khalil Bey did, when someone had an apartment such as his, why use anything aside from that apartment and those paintings to seduce women?

Khalil Bey collected other things as well. He had a Russian bear shot by Emperor Alexander, a gift from the emperor himself. Coins, inlaid chests, chessboards. He had fur coats made out of nearly every animal he could name. And books. But it was the paintings that drew the most attention. Politicians came to see his collection, artists, writers, women, gamblers—anybody Khalil Bey wanted to see would come for his collection. Whoever he wanted to meet, for whatever reason, he could. It was not only women he could seduce.

*The Origin of the World*
GUSTAVE COURBET
1866

OIL ON CANVAS
18⅛" × 21⅝"

Khalil Bey commissioned one more work from Courbet. A painting in which, a critic jokingly suggested, Courbet forgot to paint the arms, legs, and head of the model. Khalil Bey kept her in his dressing room behind a green veil.

It was said he was building a secret museum of sexuality.

She is life size, though that is not so big when you think about it.

Courbet sometimes brought visitors to see *The Origin*, but often he came alone, to learn from what he himself had done. "You don't visit me anymore," Khalil Bey joked. "You only visit her." Jo, too, came often. She had been the model once again, though this time not so recognizable.

Her body is an echo of one of Courbet's grottos. Something to be entered, explored, admired. She is her own arabesque: the curve of the sheets pushed above her breasts, the curve of her breasts, the curve of her belly, the curve of her buttocks and her thighs, the imagined curve of her interior.

Jo would stare the longest. Her body as she had never seen it. The viewer's eye drawn up along her thighs and straight inside her. Courbet had shown her a hidden part of herself; she would always defend him.

Later someone would find a painting of a head and claim it was *The Origin*'s—lopped off to protect Jo's identity. A far bigger violation than painting her without a head in the first place. Courbet would never have done it. Nor would Khalil Bey.

It is often believed that Muslims are not allowed to depict human forms in art, but that is not exactly right. Muslims are not allowed to worship human forms in art. Most of the sultans had their portraits painted. Turkish artists are known for having drawn the sultans as they were—old and tired and thin; strong and willful and handsome; sometimes too fat for their horses, which were shown to sag under their weight.

When Bellini came to paint the portrait of Mehmed II, it is said that the artist referenced *The Beheading of St. John the Baptist,* causing the sultan to complain that the painting contained anatomical inaccuracies: the neck of the decapitated was elongated when it should have been contracted. When the artist protested, the sultan is said to have had a slave brought forth and beheaded, and so was proved correct.

Then again, a similar story was told about a Greek painter, Pairhasios, and yet another similar story was told about Michelangelo.

In the end, Bellini's portrait of Mehmed II, known as Mehmed the Conqueror, for his 1453 conquest of Constantinople, was sold off in a bazaar by the sultan's son and heir, who did not approve of Western art.

Most of Khalil Bey's paintings were landscapes. But that is not how they are remembered.

Whose world is it that has found its origin in *The Origin of the World*? Courbet liked to say he wrote his autobiography in self-portraits. Others put it less kindly: "Courbet waving. Courbet walking. Courbet at a standstill. Courbet reclining. Courbet sitting. Courbet dead." Perhaps *The Origin of the World* is yet another self-portrait. There at the vanishing point, beyond where our invasive eye can travel, is Courbet conceived.

"To paint a landscape you have to truly know it," Courbet once said. It is no wonder Whistler was so angry.

The police arrived at one Courbet exhibition having heard that *The Origin of the World* would be there. They hoped to arrest Courbet on charges of obscenity, but the rumor was false. It was a painting much talked of and little seen.

When Khalil Bey auctioned his collection, *Sleep* and *The Origin of the World* sold privately to different buyers, and *The Origin of the World* disappeared. It surfaced briefly in 1899, then again in 1913, when a grainy photograph appeared.

Only now do we know that in 1945 *The Origin* was stolen by the Nazis from the Hungarian who owned it, then stolen again by the Russians and sold back to the Hungarian, who transported it to Switzerland. *The Origin* was kept in a double frame, covered by a painting called *The Castle in the Snow.*

Behind every picture there is another picture. Behind every story another story.

One Courbet work long known as *The Preparation of the Dead Girl* turned out to have originally been titled *The Preparation of the Bride.* It is an unfinished portrait of a stiff and unmoving girl having her toilette prepared by a host of helpers. It is not known how or where the painting's title got changed, though the why is perhaps obvious.

Courbet is known now for having painted things that already looked like paint. Such as snow. And flesh.

It was not until 1963 that *The Origin* was revealed to be in the possession of famed psychoanalyst and Freudian Jacques Lacan. Like the Hungarian, like Khalil Bey, Lacan kept the *Origin* hidden, this time behind a clever hilly landscape that followed the curves of Jo Hiffernan's naked and headless body, a landscape painted by Lacan's brother-in-law, the famed surrealist André Masson. Masson is known for, among other things, imposing strict and arbitrary conditions upon the creation of his art, like refusing to eat or sleep until a drawing was finished. It is said that after escaping the Nazis, who called his work "degenerate," Masson arrived in New York only to have his portfolio of drawings shredded by customs agents who called his work "pornographic."

*The Origin of the World* was not exhibited publicly until 1988, more than one hundred years after it was painted. It hangs now in the Musée d'Orsay, where patrons are often embarrassed to linger too long in front of it. Or they force themselves to stare, perhaps imagining their own faces where Jo's would be.

"She is a metaphor," Khalil Bey liked to say.

"For what?" his guests would inevitably ask.

Khalil Bey would never answer.

At least one critic insisted that *The Origin* was a portrait of a woman in orgasm. Another called her obese.

When first put on display at the Musée d'Orsay, *The Origin of the World* was placed behind armored glass. Now its postcard sales are second only to Renoir's *Bal du Moulin de la Galette*.

In 1792, Sultan Selim III had begun a series of reforms, known as the "new order," meant to modernize the ailing empire. Young Ottomans were taught French, and embassies were established in all the major cities of Europe. Thirty years later, Khalil Bey was born, learned French, became a European ambassador. The empire may have been on its last legs, but of it was born the republic.

"We cannot fear change," Khalil Bey would say in his negotiations. "We must manage it."

In the days and years after he sold his collection, which paid his debts, Khalil Bey thought sometimes of Süleyman the Magnificent, whose heart was buried on the battlefields of Hungary, though his body was buried in the grand mosque built in his name in Istanbul. Khalil Bey's paintings, it turned out, were nothing but a body. Their heart was buried in him.

With his eyes closed, Khalil Bey could still see his paintings.

After he left Paris, apparently cured of his syphilis, Khalil Bey was again a servant to the sultan, a foreign minister at home and abroad. He lived both for Egypt and the empire, one contained inside the other, much as he lived both for pleasure and for work. And when his vision first dimmed, then narrowed, he filled in any absences with his memory.

In myth, blindness can be a reward, a gift of prophecy and wisdom, or a punishment, just as death can be a reward or a punishment. An entrance into the infinite. Or an end.

When Khalil Bey died in 1877, at only forty-six, he was indeed finally blind, though he was also, in that moment, happily married and, in many ways, a contented man.

# THE GATHERING OF DESIRE

*It* was the age of automatons and already there was a fly made of brass, a mechanical tiger, an eight-foot elephant, and a duck that swallowed a piece of grain and excreted a small pellet. There was a dancing woman and a trumpet-playing man. A miniature Moscow that burned and collapsed and sprang up again.

And once there was, and once there wasn't,
in the time when magic was mystery and science was fact,
in the time when God's hand could arm man's puppet,
when miracles were seen to be believed, and schemes were believed
   to be seen,
there was the Ottoman Turk, the chess-playing mechanical man.

## Philadelphia, 1827

Outside the Turk's cabinet is the stage, the audience, and an opponent coaxed out of the crowd by Maelzel the showman. Inside the Turk's cabinet is the dim light of the candle, its smoke, which does not ventilate as quickly as it burns, the magnets and mechanics that allow S. to control the automaton's movements, the small chessboard that allows him to control the larger game. Outside the cabinet is all of the mystery and wonder and suspicions that he alone should be free of, the one person who does not have to ponder how it works—inside is a man, him. He is the Turk's beating heart, he is its brain. Its skill is his, its first move, its reactions, the many wins and few losses, all his. And yet.

Outside the cabinet, the Turk is a champion. Inside the cabinet, there are only endless moves, no trickier than the moves S. makes to slide his mechanized seat from left to right, from front to back as Maelzel the showman opens the various doors of the cabinet to prove to the audience that nobody is inside. Maelzel is a master of proving what is not true.

Still there are rumors. A boy, a dwarf, a man without legs. Some have even guessed the truth, mentioning S. by name. And yet the crowds arrive. They will not relinquish their amazement.

They have been performing in Philadelphia a month already when she comes to the stage, the last match of the night. "Never a woman before," Maelzel announces to the crowd. "Finally a woman. Can she beat the Turk? Can she?"

In the café in Paris, S. sometimes played women; sometimes they flirted with him, but rarely. His appearance was not one to draw women in, nor was his manner. It is no matter: he will play whomever.

Gone are the days of playing masters.

"What is your name, madam?" Maelzel asks, but S. does not hear her answer.


SHE TAKES THE STAGE SURPRISED. She did not mean to volunteer. Her children willed her to, she believes. The power of them together, wishing, with the same force that caused her to take them to the performance in the first place, the first time any of them have gone out since the disappearance (death, she tells herself) of her husband, their father, Thomas, eight months ago.

There have been whispers: another family, a secret debt, a sudden madness. But she does not believe them. Given a mystery, people, she finds, force startling narratives on the unlikeliest characters. Thomas was a Quaker, a teacher and reformer, a person of family; and now people want to believe him less than he was. But she does not care what they want to believe. After all her time in the faith, after all her efforts to hold their community together—it astonishes her to realize it—she does not care if she sees any of them again. Instead all of her work goes to accepting the most logical truth: she will never know what happened, and Thomas will always be gone. Every day she must convince herself of this or else she will merely pass the time waiting for his return.

Her first look at the Turk is no more than a glance. But when she looks more steadily at him, she wants to laugh—at his height, his fur-lined robes, his ridiculous turban. There is an air of the absurd to the whole occasion, playing chess on stage against an oversized toy—but she finds she feels sorry for him. His dark downcast eyes, painted on of course, make her think of a serious man forced to attend a costume party. He's sad, she thinks, before she can chase the idea away. He reminds her of Thomas on the occasions when he was forced into society and she was the one to comfort him with the thought of coming home again.

She settles in her seat, arranges her skirts, focuses on the ivory pieces in their familiar formation in front of her. She looks out into the audience, tries to see her children, but all is darkness and shadow.

Thomas Jr. is fourteen, while Margaret is eleven, but in recent months they have twinned themselves. During meals they stare across the table, one at the other, refusing any longer to eat meat and pretending—yes, pretending, she is certain—that they are able to communicate without speech. They take long walks by themselves, and force her to wait through long silences before they will answer any question. They all live now in her father's house; she herself sleeps in the room she had as a child, a strange comfort, and the children have two small rooms adjacent to each other, with a door in between. At night she can hear them talking across the divide, though as much as she strains, she cannot make out what they say. During the days they frequently close themselves in one room or the other, and though she stands often outside the door, it is so quiet that she feels forbidden to enter or even knock.

She has thought sometimes of sending Thomas Jr. away to school.

Perhaps she is jealous. They have each other.

But she is their mother; it is grounded in love, her concern.

She herself has stopped going to meetings, no longer calls on anyone, rarely receives calls from anyone; she has refused all invitations for missions and canceled those that were already scheduled. Perhaps her children's strangeness is merely a reflection of her own. She cannot seem to move forward in her old life, nor determine how to begin anew.

"Madam will have the first move," Maelzel says, though she knows that is not the Turk's custom. It is because she is a woman, she assumes, but she does not argue.

It was Thomas who taught the children chess, and after his disappearance (death, she tells herself) it was her father who taught her, when she and the children moved into his house, when it became clear that Thomas was not returning and that she needed both shelter and a job, and her father had, so gently, offered both. Now the four of them play long tournaments, the only thing to reliably keep the children in her presence.

She had thought she was a good mother. Before.

She studies the pieces, imagines the game ahead. She wants very much to win. For them, she thinks, so they will be proud of her. She should find it wrong, she knows, to want so much, to be on this stage even, but it is hard to believe now that God would concern himself with such things.

She is embarrassed to see her hand quiver as she raises it over the board, but thankfully only Maelzel is close enough to notice. She glances up at him, and he smiles.

"Do not worry, madam, he has not leapt at anyone yet," he announces loudly, and the crowd laughs.

How angry people make her lately. She constantly wishes for more grace, but finds herself failing daily at the task of merely being kind. Only her father is still patient with her.

It has been a surprise to her, how grief has changed her.

She takes a breath. Makes her first move. Waits for the Turk to make his.

THERE WAS ONCE an Ottoman city of seven hills, of three seas, of four hundred fountains, and within that city was another city of fulfilled desires. Within that second city was a pleasure house encircled by a garden of wild tulips where shot into the earth was an army of arrows that had arced over the wall in flight from the bows of a tribe of men driven mad by love. To the east, there was a river valley, once a desert, flooded by their tears.

The Turk knows there is a kind of desire that causes roses to bloom.

At least, once there was.

EACH NIGHT, BY THIS HOUR, S. is curved in on himself, shoulders bent forward, legs bent upward. His fingers claw over the pieces, his eyes track the magnets and the moves, and his mind is nearly curled in on itself.

He had thought he would travel. Instead he is in a space barely larger than himself, forbidden to talk of his work, left with only Maelzel and the mechanical man as his companions. When all options were open to him, he desired only chess, but now that only chess is open to him, he desires everything else.

This loss pains him more than any other. Each night he thinks he will quit.

It is the heat, the smoke, the endless games; they are inside of him just as he is inside of the Turk, and they press to be released just as he does.

He makes his move, and above him the Turk responds.

THERE IS A WIND, the Lodos, that rises from the south and reverses the currents of the three seas. There are citizens so consumed by the Lodos that they believe they have been driven mad. Using the excuse of their madness, they speak plainly to those they love, but because they are believed to be mad, their words are not believed.

The Turk knows that the language of madness is not far from other languages, including the language of love.

He knows there were once Ottomans so versed in love they spoke only in poetry.

SHE IS A FAST PLAYER. Early in her lessons she memorized whole games, delighting even the children with her quick mind. More than one new side to her has been discovered, not all bad, since Thomas's disappearance (death, she tells herself). She knows she should not have pride, that she should not put stock in games. But she knows, too, that this, now, is what she has, and if she does not take pleasure from somewhere, if she does not find ways to stay close to her children, she will have nothing.

She and the Turk exchange piece after piece, motion after motion. Finally she is focused, and does not think of the children or her husband or even the magical mechanics of the figure opposite her.

AT FIRST THERE IS a rhythm and S. is relieved to realize he will last the night. He had expected she would be slow and her concentration would lead to his own distraction. But then she is quick and he finds himself responding even more quickly, as if it is a race and he is pushing her forward faster and faster, and then maybe she is pushing him or it is some other force altogether, because finally, he makes a mistake.

S. is a master; he cannot believe what he has done. Has he done it? He lifts his hand and looks at it in the light of the candle. His breathing first stops, then comes quicker.

Outside S. is the next move, the lifting of the magnets, the shifting of gears that give S.'s motion to the Turk's hand; but inside S. is the growing sense that inside of his self is some other self. S. turns his hand over, palm up, and imagines above him the Turk, too, turning his hand over, palm up. S. holds his hand still and feels an overwhelming desire to move it. He feels the Turk's desire. I am possessed, he thinks. God help me, I am possessed. The feeling grows inside of him, an invading conqueror, the Turk the Turk the Turk.

SHE SEES IT IMMEDIATELY. Automatically she looks up at the Turk's painted eyes, but of course they reveal nothing. She looks out at the audience, but they cannot see, do not understand what has happened. Even Maelzel, who sometimes paces the stage and sometimes stands behind her and sometimes fusses with a crank at the side of the cabinet, as if he is adjusting the machinery, does not seem to notice.

She cannot be contained.

I will beat him, she thinks.

OPPOSITE HER, for long minutes the Turk sits motionless, as if in thought. Finally Maelzel declares the game suspended until the next night. "The machine must get its rest," he says with a flourish that draws, from the audience, a loud laugh. Nobody asks her if she can return the next night, but of course she will.

Maelzel, with barely a look at her, escorts her down the stairs, and she joins the crowd exiting the theater. People congratulate her as she walks among them. Some smile, some stare, some do not seem to realize she has been their entertainment and stare instead at those who greet her. "Thank you," she says over and over, but all she can think is, Tomorrow, I will beat him tomorrow.

The children await her at the front of the theater, and immediately they, too, come undone.

"We saw Father," they say in unison and she, already excited, feels a flush come over her.

"Here?" she says.

"Of course," Thomas Jr. says. "Couldn't you see him?"

She looks first at him, then his sister. There are people and carriages and horses crowding the streets and sidewalk, but they do not notice any of it. They are euphoric. "What do you mean?" she says.

"He was standing behind you. On the stage. Couldn't you tell?"

"There was no one there," she says. "Except that man, Maelzel."

"Father was there," Margaret says. "We saw him."

"It's what we've been hoping for," Thomas Jr. says. "What we've been working toward. A manifestation."

"Come," she says, grabbing each of them by the hand so quickly that they are too surprised to avoid her grasp. "We are going home."

"Where you'll be punished," she says as she pulls them down the street. "That is not what we believe," she says, though even as she says it she hears Thomas's voice: "We cannot tell them what to think. We can only teach them how."

It is as if the children have conjured him after all.

"HE IS MAKING ME LOSE," S. insists, and Maelzel looks at him with bemused concern.

"Perhaps we should cancel the next evening's entertainment," Maelzel says. "You do not seem well."

"He is controlling the game. I cannot do what I want."

"Rest now. You will feel differently in the morning. Or perhaps Georges can play in your stead."

S. points a trembling finger at Maelzel. "Do not replace me," he shouts.

And then, more calmly: "I will not let her win just because she is a woman. No matter how beautiful."

"She is perfectly ordinary," Maelzel says. "And nobody has suggested that you let her win. Play the game!" he says in a burst of anger.

S. lowers his gaze.

"She's quite good, isn't she?" Maelzel says. "That's what has got you so disturbed, isn't it?"

"He is in love with her," S. says, turning away, though not quickly enough to avoid hearing Maelzel's sharp laugh.

"Perhaps you have begun to confuse yourself with the machine," Maelzel calls out, but S. turns again and says crisply, "I have not," before walking away.

"THERE IS SURELY a man inside," her father says, when she mentions the Turk's mistake. They are downstairs, by the fire, the children upstairs. She has abandoned them while she ponders what to do.

"What makes you think so?" she asks.

"Because mistakes are human. They are not godly and they are not mechanical."

"Machines make mistakes."

"Machines break. They do not make mistakes."

He is right, she realizes. It is the only logical explanation. Her father and the children often puzzled over the mystery of the automaton, her father arguing for mechanical genius and the children arguing for God's creation. She herself, when pressed to choose a side, would only say, "It is a mystery." It had been a mystery she was willing to live with.

"Are you disappointed?" she asks.

"Maybe a little," her father admits. "But still, to imagine how man could invent such a thing . . . it's remarkable."

"Should I tell the children?" she asks, but her father shrugs.

"Maybe they do not need to know," he says.

"They think they saw Thomas. At the theater."

Her father flinches, then tries quickly not to show that he has.

There had been a time when she thought she would not marry; her mother had died so young, and her father, she'd assumed, would need looking after in his old age. But it was her father who had encouraged her to marry Thomas, who'd hired him as a clerk at his bookshop; and it was her father who had helped Thomas with the children when she traveled on missions, often for weeks at a time. The two of them must have shared so many moments that she did not even know of. And yet for months, her father had let her sadness take precedence over his own.

"Perhaps they saw someone who looked like him?" her father says. "Even I have been struck, many times, by people with a resemblance."

"They believe they saw him onstage. A manifestation, they called it. They think they summoned him." "I cannot tell them what to believe," she continues. "But they should not be allowed to lie."

"They are grieving."

"As am I," she says angrily. And then more quietly: "As are you."

Her father leans forward as if about to speak, but then he leans back again and says nothing.

"What?" she asks.

"I do not know if I should tell you this. I had decided not to, but now I think I was wrong."

She waits.

"There was a body. Many months ago. It was disfigured and I couldn't be certain, so I didn't mention it."

"That was kind of you," she says without moving. "You have borne so much of my burden."

"He wore Thomas's watch and his rings." Her father pauses. "But I could not bear to identify him by his belongings rather than his face."

"Oh," she says. She is surprised to realize it does matter. There has been a body all this time. Thomas is truly dead. She tries to stop the tears, but cannot. "I'm sorry," she says. "It was kind of you."

"I know it was absurd," her father says, "but all I could think was if only he would speak, then I could be certain it was him."

"It's all right, Father," she says. "I understand."

"I'm afraid there's more," her father says, and he waits while she collects herself. "He had been dead only a few days."

She cannot for a moment understand what he is saying, but then she realizes. "How long was he missing before he died?" she asks.

"At least a month."

"Oh," she says again, but this time she does not cry. "Oh," she says again.

Her father never remarried after her mother died during the yellow fever, though surely he could have. How dear he is to her. How hard it must have been to see what he saw.

"What did you do with the body?" she asks as quietly as she can.

"He is buried in my grave," her father says, and a sob overtakes him. Quickly she drops to her knees at his feet, and leans her cheek against his knee.

"I'm grateful," she says over and over. "I'm so grateful." And when she cries it is at the thought that one day she will no longer have him, and it seems as if all that is ahead of her is one grief and then another.

THEY WERE CHILDREN TOGETHER, she and Thomas. And then had come the day, at nine years old, when she received the inward light, the word of God. (Had she really? Still she wonders.) And everyone in the meeting, including Thomas, witnessed it, and afterward, she went with her mother on one mission after another, the child who so early in life received God's attention, until the day her mother died, and she continued the missions alone, only fourteen years old at the time.

She could not herself remember the moment—not even falling to the floor or coming to in her father's arms. The closest she could come was the next morning when she woke in her parents' bed, a place she had never before been. She was alone and it was late morning. Her chores, minor as they were, had been done for her—the breakfast dishes washed, the bedrooms dusted. It was the kind of gentle treatment reserved for the ill, and so she lay in her parents' bed, afraid, until finally her mother came looking for her, told her how she would accompany her on her next mission. "You've been called, just like I was, though much younger," her mother said. And that had been all the discussion she ever had about what became her life's work, traveling to other Quaker meetings and testifying, or more often sitting quietly, wondering if God had really entered her, and if he had, why he wouldn't let her remember.

When she and Thomas met again, years later, when he went to work in her father's bookshop, where Thomas began his school, he told her what he remembered. "You went bright red, like a hot brick, and you fell to the ground, and you quivered. And your expression, it was . . . I can't describe it," he said. "You were a living angel. Everybody said so."

How strange it seems to her now. How long she believed herself special, until the very moment Thomas disappeared, and she saw how little reason—how little meaning—there was at all.

She misses him. She had lived off Thomas's belief, it seems, and without him, her belief is gone. It was Thomas who was special—she always understood that; she drew so much from him, from the things he taught the children. His own desire for God's word, for the inward light, which he never received, had made him stronger, she knows. If only she could learn from him again.

SHE TELLS THE CHILDREN GENTLY: their father is certainly dead, and tomorrow they will visit where he is buried.

It is Margaret who answers first. "But of course he is dead," she says. "That is how we've been speaking to him."

"Did you think he was alive?" Thomas Jr. says kindly, like the little gentleman he had been eight months ago.

The children have been, it turns out, studying books on death and reincarnation and spirits, ones they somehow snuck out of the shop, and they have been conducting séances on their own in this room.

She wants to tuck the children into their beds, to climb into her own, but when they offer to conduct a séance for her, she does not stop them. They are happy as they show her, Thomas Jr. especially. It is a relief to them, it seems, to call a truce with her. They clear a space on the floor, and the three of them sit. Margaret lights a candle, and Thomas Jr. pulls from his pockets a handkerchief stained with ink, a pen, and a folded piece of paper with his father's writing on it.

She feels the urge to snatch the objects up and hide them away, to press her lips to them in secret, but she has many of Thomas's belongings, and not one of them has truly been a comfort to her.

Where had he been the month before he died? How can she remove this new image of him—wandering, beaten, rotten— from her mind?

She almost cries out at the surprise of Thomas Jr.'s touch as he says, "Take my hand, Mother."

"You don't have to be frightened," Margaret says, taking her other hand. "We only raise friendly spirits."

She is surprised again when it is Margaret who leads, calling out "to the beyond."

"Margaret is a better conductor," Thomas Jr. whispers when his mother glances at him.

When her daughter speaks again, it is in a false voice, deep and ridiculous.

She is embarrassed to realize she was hoping to hear Thomas's voice.

"Who are you?" Thomas Jr. asks, and Margaret replies, "I am the keeper of the dead."

It is a phrase she recognizes from one of Margaret's favorite stories. The child is pretending, she thinks.

"Have you seen Father?" Thomas Jr. asks. "Is he well?"

"Yes," Margaret says. "Very well. He was so pleased to see you. He is so glad you, too, are well."

"Will you tell him we feel the same?" Thomas Jr. says, his voice tremulous.

"Of course," his sister says in her false voice.

She stares at Margaret, who glances first at her, then at Thomas Jr., who has his eyes closed and a beatific smile on his face. Her daughter turns back to her and smiles sheepishly. She understands then. Margaret is not playing a game but comforting her older brother in the manner that works best.

It is a chance for conspiracy, she realizes. And yet she snatches her hands away. "Stop it," she says. "You are making a fool of him," she says to Margaret, who stares at her open-mouthed. "You are letting her make a fool of you," she says to Thomas Jr., who looks sullen now. Angry again.

"She's not ready to believe," Margaret says to Thomas Jr. "Don't listen to her—she just isn't ready to believe."

Thomas Jr. nods, and the children silently gather their things from the floor. It is as if they pity her.

How could she have done it?

They are compassionate children. They worried so over the orphans who died in the asylum fire some years ago. And more recently over the colored boys who were kidnapped, and believed sold South. They have their father in them, she knows.

"I'm sorry," she says. "You are right. I do not know what to believe."

Thomas Jr. is folding the piece of paper with his father's writing on it when she takes it from his hand.

They stand waiting, heads down, while she reads it.

"Where did you get this?"

She looks first at one child, then the other, but neither will look at her.

"It is from one of Father's journals, isn't it?"

Thomas had asked her long ago to grant him one privacy, to not read what he did not invite her to, and she had sworn that she wouldn't. And yet he was gone but two days before she went to his journals, only to find them missing from their shelves.

"We didn't read it," Thomas Jr. says. "We just tore out the last page. It was the last thing he wrote." He sobs then, and in an instant, little Margaret gathers her brother to her small chest.

She cannot bear to stand outside their circle, and so she clutches them both to her, the page still in her hand.

When they have all calmed themselves, the children bring her the stack of journals they had hidden, and she takes each of them by the hand and kisses them, and then ushers them to bed.

"You know I miss your father," she says, standing in the doorway between them. "You know it is almost unbearable to me to have lost him. But it would be so much worse to lose you."

"Can we still have séances?" Thomas Jr. asks, and both children watch her as they wait.

What is the right thing? She wants so much to comfort

them. She looks particularly at Margaret, who is studying her with a face of open curiosity.

"Yes," she says finally, and the children rise out of their beds with joy, directly into her arms.

It is a while before, journals in hand, she searches out her father, to ask him to do what she cannot.

S. DREAMS OF HER ALL NIGHT. Awake or asleep, he cannot stop imagining her. He believes she has bewitched the Turk and the Turk has bewitched him. He knows this is impossible, understands even the mechanical workings of the machine, and yet, against his own will, he believes it. In the night, he lifts his hand out from the bedcovers and turns it over and back again, imagining somewhere the Turk is doing the same. You are at my command, he thinks. He reaches out his hand, feels his fingers unfurl, but what he sees is the Turk's hand reaching out, touching her cheek, caressing it.

IN THE CITY OF SEVEN HILLS, three seas, and four hundred fountains, there is a story the Turk wishes he could tell, of love.

The beautiful daughter of an ordinary man, Leyla was a child when she met Mejnun, the son of a powerful chief, and they played together without the notice of their parents, until one day Leyla's mother saw how often they chose each other's company and was troubled by such intense affection between two so young. She sent Mejnun away, intending for their separation to be brief, a test, but soon Mejnun was appearing outside Leyla's house at odd hours, not knocking but staring into windows and climbing the wall of the house's garden just to look over the edge. He was sent away again, and then again, and then told finally to stay away for good.

He fled to the desert, where he wandered.

During this time, Mejnun's father begged Leyla's parents to allow the two to marry, but her parents would not marry their daughter to a madman. So Mejnun's father carried Mejnun out of the desert to be treated, but upon receiving his cure, Mejnun begged God to increase his love and he escaped again to the desert. Again his father found him, brought him home, and again Mejnun sought the desert, the only place large enough to house his love.

Leyla, too, was faithful. She kept to the interiors, walled inside her garden, where she would sing songs of Mejnun's invention.

In the desert, Mejnun met a crow and asked it to relay the message of his love to his love, and in her garden, Leyla heard Mejnun's song of love sung by a crow.

In the desert, Mejnun heard the wind and asked it to relay the message of his love to his love, and Leyla, in her garden, heard it.

In the desert, Mejnun met an old woman and asked her to bind him in chains, to pretend they were beggars—to be beggars—so they could approach Leyla's house unnoticed. But when the old woman did as he asked, and they entered Leyla's house as beggars, and he glimpsed the object of his love, all Mejnun could do was break his chains and run to the desert, where his love was housed.

Finally Leyla married another, but she would not allow her husband any right but the right to look at her.

When Mejnun's father died, his tomb was watered with Mejnun's tears.

When Mejnun's mother died, roses sprouted from her grave.

Leyla arranged to meet Mejnun in her garden, but he refused to let her see him, and so they each remained hidden, a small distance between them, while Mejnun recited a poem of his love for his love.

"Mejnun," Leyla said.

But Mejnun would not speak her name.

"Your name is inside of mine," he said, "like the fruit inside its skin. There it is protected."

When Leyla's husband died and Leyla's time of mourning passed, she arranged to meet Mejnun again. Mejnun entered her room, and they stepped, for the first time, into an embrace, but Mejnun fled again to the desert, calling out behind him that he carried her with him.

His love for her had grown so large it could only be contained by all things.

In the end, Leyla fell ill and died, and upon her tomb, Mejnun died.

But many have dreamt of them together in paradise.

The Turk knows that inside each of us is a black light and a love without end. He wishes he could tell her so.

THE NEXT NIGHT the game resumes, and since she cannot see the opponent she now believes is hidden somewhere, she directs her gaze at the Turk. Straight at his downcast eyes she looks, willing them to turn upward. She believes she is somehow challenging the man in control. (Could he really be inside?) She believes he can see through the Turk's eyes, but as she stares she is overcome first by a sense of unease and then by a sense of familiarity. The same feeling she would have when she was in one room and could hear Thomas in another.

She shudders, and then she feels her breath rise inside of her, a moment of desire.

Thomas, she thinks, and she looks over her shoulder, only to see Maelzel staring back. Thomas? And then it is as if she can feel him emanating from the machine opposite her.

Have I been playing Thomas? she thinks.

How can she consider such a thing? She is not the kind of person to consider such a thing. And yet she does.

It is the children. They have gotten to her with their stories.

IT IS THE BEGINNING of the night and S. should be fresh, not yet discomfited, but he cannot relieve himself of the feelings of the night before. He is hot already, fevered yet again; his mind is pitched fast against concentration. He is all of the things he formerly told his students not to be: distracted, rushed, and too much in need of winning.

Perhaps in France there is some unchosen life S. can still return to. If he was to expose Maelzel, it would be a sensation. His name would be everywhere, he would be recognized as a great master, the man who beat so many masters, but he would also be known as a cheat and a charlatan. Perhaps there is money in the story, but money has never satisfied him. If only he could tell somebody. He has grown so disdainful of people, of the ease with which they can be fooled.

She is going to beat him; he would like her to know that she beat a master. He would tell her, too, that the Turk wanted her to win.

But how can he tell her both things—that he was the master and the Turk was as well? How can he believe both things?

SHE FINDS HERSELF wanting to laugh. Could the afterlife be something so ridiculous as an eternity inside a machine playing a game against all comers? It hardly seems likely. Perhaps her father, the avid chess player, would enjoy such an eternal existence, but Thomas? No. But perhaps he wanted to reach her—or the children—and this was the only way. Or perhaps—she wants to laugh again—she is losing her sense. Her lack of sleep has affected her rationale.

It is possible she loved Thomas more than she loved God, she realizes. And perhaps this is her punishment. She is to be without both.

But what if she chooses simply to believe? To lay claim to the idea as a fact: Thomas has visited her, and their children, and he has done it out of love and a desire to see them again, to know they are well and surviving.

Why not let that be a comfort to her?

SHE READ ONLY the one page torn from Thomas's journal. "I know what I hear and yet I know I cannot be hearing it," he had written. "I know I am sane and yet I feel as if I cannot be. God has spoken to me at last, and yet the things he says. The things I now know. I am the man in the story, whispering to the reeds, 'King Midas has ass's ears.'"

Her father read the rest and said only, "I think perhaps Thomas was ill."

"How well he hid it," she said, and her father nodded.

"It seems impossible," she said.

And yet it wasn't.

S. IS HOT WITH FEVER. His hands are trembling. He thinks that nothing is his own anymore. He cannot control his thoughts, let alone his actions. Perhaps inside of him is another man controlling him, and inside of him another man controlling him, and so on.

"Stop it," he says aloud, and he believes surely the crowd has heard him, but there is only silence in response.

How would it feel, he wonders, to sit in a chair and play the Turk. To sit opposite him and watch the hand extend, grasp its piece, make its move.

He longs for it.

The audience thinks the Turk is the body and somewhere hidden from sight is the soul; but, S. knows, he has become the body, and the Turk is the soul. Together perhaps he and the Turk are a complete man—but no longer is he such a thing when they are apart. He can no longer hold himself together.

If people were to believe that the Turk's magic was real, they would burn him, drown him, destroy him. What they want is to choose to believe in something they know is not real. An easy kind of faith. One they can control. S. does not have this comfort any longer.

He looks one last time at the small chessboard. He cannot

win unless she makes her own mistake, something she has not done during their several hours of play. He leans his head back against the cabinet interior. He pinches out the candle's small flame with his thumb and forefinger. He will not make another move, not even to exit. Maelzel shall have to drag him out.

Perhaps she will be the one to rescue him, to pull his head onto her lap, where it will nestle deep in her skirts while he lies with his eyes closed, refusing to look up at her.

He should not have extinguished the candle; instead, he should have used it to light a flame and burn the Turk to cinders. He wishes he could be disassembled and folded into a crate, as the Turk so regularly is.

In Paris, S.'s opponents had watched his hands, followed his eyes. He had wished, so many times, to be invisible.

Now, in the dark, a peace comes over him. He thinks he can smell her perfume. He is suffused. He can feel her across from him and he wants nothing more than to reach out and take her hand, so that the warmth from it spreads through him.

How can he have gone so long without love?

SHE SEES THE MOVE and yet she struggles to bring herself to make it.

She wants some kind of sign. Proof. She wants to know that Thomas is healed.

Maybe it is not Thomas's absence she must live with, but this new presence. She looks at the long fingers of the Turk, which have reached out and moved each piece. She imagines taking him by the hand and warming his fingers with her own. Perhaps her father is right. It does not matter if there is anyone or anything inside. She should simply be amazed at man's creation.

What she misses most about Thomas is the way he spoke to her. He would inspire such thoughts in her. Perhaps she and the children can do that for each other.

She makes her last move, and the game is hers. The crowd cheers, somewhere in the room her children leap to their feet, even Maelzel congratulates her, and still the machine keeps his eyes cast down, as if studying the board to determine the cause of his loss.

WHAT THE TURK WISHES he could make her understand is she is not Leyla, left behind. She is Mejnun.

Inside of her is the capacity to love beyond love.

Inside of her is the history of time up until this moment.

Inside of her is an infinite space that contains all things, including what she has lost.

What he wishes he could make her understand is there is no her, there is only inside of her.

How he wishes he could tell her.

# ACKNOWLEDGMENTS

A graduate student of mine once turned to me and said, "I hate acknowledgments pages." I knew instantly what he meant; I, too, despite being a voracious reader of acknowledgments, sometimes hate them. Because from the outside, they can feel like a statement of the worst of the writing world—the who-you-knows, the what-you-wons, the where-you've-beens, the students-of. But from the inside, when you are the grateful one, hyperaware of how your book would not exist without the whos, the whats, the wheres, the thought of not writing an acknowledgments page (and I did think of it) is actually painful. So:

It took me nearly ten years to write this book. You can imagine how many people and places that entailed. I hope to thank each of you in person.

But especially:

Julie Barer, my agent, and Alane Salierno Mason, my editor, have proven to be two of the smartest, most literary, most ethical businesspeople I have ever met. I am proud to be represented by the Book Group and published by Norton, two institutions that value books not just as products but as experiences, as ideas, as art. Equal gratitude to Nicole Cunningham and Ashley Patrick for so much boots-on-the-ground work.

Mary Kenagy Mitchell and Andy Furman read nearly every one of these stories, sometimes more than once. A writer is lucky to have one great reader; I have two.

My colleagues (past and present) at Florida Atlantic University have become not just my friends but my family. Folks sometimes wonder why creative writing is in the English department, but many of these stories grew out of my understanding of my colleagues' scholarship and writing. If I have a muse, it is the FAU Department of English.

I'm also grateful to the FAU Dorothy F. Schmidt College of Arts and Letters, the Millay Colony for the Arts, the Betsy Hotel, and the Studios of Key West for support as I wrote these stories.

Most of all, thank you to the other Bucaks: my parents; my big brother, Deniz; my sister-in-law, Gabrielle; and my niece and nephew, Audrey and Devin, who are my two favorite people, the two funniest, smartest, most interesting people I could ever spend time with, and who I wish I could see every day.

Finally, special gratitude to the magazines and editors that first published a number of these stories:

"The History of Girls" in Witness and the O. Henry Prize Stories 2013

"A Cautionary Tale" in the *Pinch*

"The Gathering of Desire" in *Normal School*

"Little Sister and Emineh" in *Prairie Schooner*

"An Ottoman's Arabesque" in the *Kenyon Review*

"Iconography" in the *Iowa Review* and the *2014 Pushcart Prize*

Many of the stories in this collection include fictionalized versions of real people and real events. My copy editor did her absolute best to keep me honest—any mistakes or misrepresentations are my own.

# CREDITS

"A Cautionary Tale." *The Pinch* 35.2 (Fall 2015).

"An Ottoman's Arabesque." *Kenyon Review* 36.2 (Spring 2014): 29–47.

"The Gathering of Desire" was originally published under the title "The Missing Beloved, The Gathering of Desire." *The Normal School* 6.2 (2013): 6–14.

"Little Sister and Emineh." *Prairie Schooner* 86.4 (2012): 83–94.

"Iconography." *The Iowa Review.* 42.2 (2012): 53-62. Reprinted in *2014 Pushcart Prize*. Ed. Bill Henderson. New York: Pushcart Press. pp. 274–284.

"The History of Girls." *Witness* 25.1 (2012): 26–36. Reprinted in *2013 O. Henry Prize Stories*. Ed. Laura Furman. New York: Anchor/ Doubleday. pp. 353–366. Reprinted *Aster(ix)*. May 31, 2016. <http:// asterixjournal.com/the-history-of-girls/>. Reprinted *Sampsonia Way*. August 4, 2016. <http://www.sampsoniaway.org/asterix -journal/2016/08/04/the-history-of-girls/>.